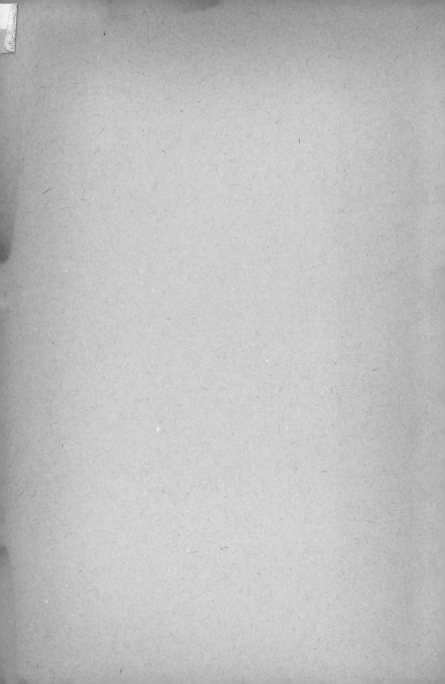

JUDY, PATROL LEADER

by

DOROTHEA MOORE

THE CHILDREN'S PRESS
LONDON AND GLASGOW

PRINTED AND MADE IN GREAT BRITAIN

CONTENTS

CHAPTER I

JUDY TURNS UP

MR. JAMES BETHUNE, Classical Master at St. Oswyth's, the principal girls' school at Merchester, had just brought his last Latin lesson for the day to an end, amid a sigh of relief from almost the entire class, a sigh that was audible.

Mr. James Bethune was perfectly aware that St. Oswyth's to a girl loathed Latin, and the knowledge did not make him any happier, as he wrestled with false quantities and the incorrect use of the ablative. But jobs had been hard to get after the War, especially to a man who limped and was mainly responsible for the upkeep of an orphan niece in the Orkneys, and Mr. James Bethune stuck to St. Oswyth's, and the two dull rooms in a house next door, where one, Mrs. Petticum, "did for him," as she phrased it, with a minimum of trouble to herself and comfort for her lodger.

Mr. James Bethune explained in his tired gentle voice to a bored IV. A., the preparation he wished done before his next class, said "Good-evening" to the girls, and went out, perfectly aware that Claire Winslow, the mimic of the form, would hardly wait till he was out of earshot to imitate his rather hesitating manner of correcting mistakes. He was afraid of girls, and they very well knew it.

With a stack of exercise books under one arm, Mr.

James Bethune limped across the hard court, where the girls, roller skating, hardly bothered to get out of his way; across a gravel path and out through a side gate. There was only a wall between the comfortable dimensions of the St. Oswyth's garden and the narrow frame of gravel walk into which Carlton House, Mrs. Petticum's chaste abode, was neatly fitted. But there was no door between, and the classical master had quite a round to make, whether he approached the lodging house, all he had for a home, by the front or the back, on his way from St. Oswyth's.

It was by the back that he approached it now, and he did that advisedly, because it had been raining heavily, and Mrs. Petticum remembered it for days if muddy boots came anywhere near the worn-out drugget that glorified the front stairs, distinguishing them from the carpetless back.

As he came into the back passage he paused involuntarily, for Mrs. Petticum, standing at the front door, which she nearly filled, was talking at the top of a voice which was seldom really hushed, to somebody presumably upon the doorstep; though Mr. James Bethune could naturally see nothing but the landlady's exceptionally broad back.

"No visitors is expected, miss; nor wanted! Yes, Mr. Bethune lives 'ere, but he knows better than to be expecting young ladies to visit him, not if they're twenty nieces!"

Mr. James Bethune forgot his muddy boots, and moved forward, feeling worried. Clearly some girl was asking for him, and that probably meant a "rag" of some kind, and a "rag" is not an attractive idea to a tired man of forty-two years, with a pile of Latin exercises to correct before bedtime. But Mr. James Bethune had been able to write D.S.O. after his name in the days of the War, and he would not run away, even from a schoolgirl.

"Anybody wanting me, Mrs. Petticum?" he asked, going forward, and Mrs. Petticum turned a wrathful and inflamed countenance that made him shrink inwardly, with a vision of unappetising meals served to a ceaseless accompaniment of "nagging" for weeks to come.

"Anybody wanting you, Mr. Bethune? You may well ask. Here's a young lady, says she's your niece and come to stay. A likely story!—as though I would have anybody's nieces 'ere!"

Mrs. Petticum had moved a little towards poor Mr. Bethune, as she emphasised her disapproval of the whole proceeding, and her movement left the front door undefended.

A small slim girl made a dart past her, and held out her hand to James Bethune. "Hallo, Uncle Jimmy, you haven't changed as much as I have," she assured him cheerfully. "I'm your niece, Jacobina; Judy to my friends, though."

Mr. James Bethune nearly dropped all the exercise books in his bewilderment.

"But Jacobina—Judy, I mean—why aren't you in Scotland?" he asked, trying hard only to sound puzzled, not dismayed.

"Oh, didn't Mrs. M'Kay's letter tell you?" Judy said innocently. "She had to go at once, you see; so—I've come here to live. You don't mind, do you?"

"Mind? Of course not, my dear child. I am simply delighted to see you," he declared valiantly and untruthfully. "You must tell me what has happened, for I assure you that I have heard nothing from Mrs. M'Kay; and Mrs. Petticum"—he turned pleadingly to that unresponsive lady—"Mrs. Petticum will, I am sure, be so kind as to see about a room for you."

The snort of Mrs. Petticum was quite a masterpiece.

CHAPTER II

SHE GETS BUSY

In Mr. Bethune's dingy and depressing sitting-room, where the dirty white tablecloth, covering half the table, never came off between his breakfast and supper, the two faced each other.

What Mr. Bethune saw was a girl of fourteen, who was small for her age, but exceptionally pretty; with a mop of wavy brown hair, bobbed, and eyes that were of a vivid blue, and held laughter in them, and a little slim upright figure that was full of life and movement. She was dressed in rather a shabby tweed coat and tam, which last she pulled off like a boy as she came into the room.

What Jacobina, alias Judy, saw was a thin man, with nice eyes, and hair growing grey on the temples, who looked tired and in need of brushing and of something else as well. He smiled as he met her direct glance.

"Satisfied it is your uncle, Judy? I don't suppose you really remember me, do you? It's six years."

"You were a bit browner about the face and the hair, I think," Judy mentioned, with an infectious little laugh. "I hope that isn't impolite, Uncle Jimmy! But, of course, I remember you. Wonder if you can say the same?"

"Of course you've grown," Mr. Bethune acknowledged. "Not so very much though. Are you really fourteen, Judy?"

"Fact," Judy told him crisply. "Quite old enough to

keep your house, Uncle Jimmy—and, do you know if you won't think me rude, it could do with just a little keeping.   Your housekeeper——"

Mr. James Bethune began to feel slightly giddy.   "My dear child, you mustn't run away with the idea that this is my house.   It is no such thing—I just lodge here, and Mrs. Petticum——"

"Is your landlady.   Oh, I see—that's why she disapproved of me," Judy said.

"I'm sure she didn't disapprove of you," Mr. Bethune assured her mendaciously.   "She was perhaps a little surprised for the moment—but you haven't told me yet why you and Mrs. M'Kay——"

"Oh, sorry," Judy told him.   "May I stir the fire—for I've really known you more than seven years, haven't I? though it's chiefly from your topping letters at birthdays and Christmas; and then may I take off my coat and sit down and tell you about it?"

"My dear child, of course!"   Mr. Bethune was shocked at having neglected the duties of hospitality.   "Let me pull up this chair and help you off with your coat. Dear me! You must be very tired after that tremendous journey.   I wonder if Mrs. Petticum could manage a cup of tea?"

Judy sat down in the springless horse-hair chair that her uncle had drawn up to the smouldering coke fire. She looked very small in her little straight blue serge frock.

"Oh, don't worry about me, Uncle Jimmy.   I can make myself some tea in two secs, if Mrs. Petticum will loan me a kettle.   But perhaps as you didn't get Mrs. M'Kay's letter I'd better tell you first why I've landed on you."

Mr. Bethune dumped his books on the table, and came and sat down opposite his niece. That she had landed on him was obvious enough. The why of it would probably include "how long?" and Mr. Bethune thought it would be well to know the worst before facing the inevitable battle with Mrs. Petticum which he foresaw and dreaded.

"Mrs. M'Kay thought you would get the letter last night, or at least this morning," Judy explained apologetically; "and she hoped it wouldn't inconvenience you very much, but she knew you must be at home because it was term time——"

"But what did she say in the letter which I ought to have had last night, or this morning, and didn't?" poor Mr. Bethune wanted to know.

"Well, she just explained that she had been obliged to go off at a moment's notice to nurse her son's baby in the Malay States," Judy told him. "The cable said his wife had died, and could she come to the baby? She is pretty certain she'll stay and look after them both, instead of bringing the baby home."

"Do you mean that Mrs. M'Kay won't be able to have you with her any longer?"

"That's the ticket," Judy told him very cheerfully. "But do you know, Uncle Jimmy, I think it's quite a good thing, really; though I hated leaving Mrs. M'Kay, of course. But fourteen isn't a kid, and I think it's time I did something for you, instead of just taking your money to keep me with Mrs. M'Kay. She thought that, too, and she said my education wouldn't be any bother, as you live next door to a girls' school."

"That's true—there's only a wall between; I will go over presently and see Miss Salway," Mr. Bethune murmured, seeing a ray of light in the darkness. "I rather think she has a vacancy, and, being so near, you could come to tea with me on Sundays. I dare say Mrs. Petticum——"

"Oh, but I should only go as a day-girl. I'm going to stay here and look after you," his niece assured him calmly. "What would be the use of only coming to tea on Sundays, Uncle Jimmy, dear? I shouldn't be able to do any mending then."

"But Mrs. Petticum mends for me," began Mr. Bethune rather desperately, and paused, not knowing how to explain further with unkindness to the small but determined niece opposite in the springless horse-hair chair.

"Does she?" asked Judy in doubt, and as she said it Mrs. Petticum marched into the room, bearing a tray before her like a sort of battering ram. There was war in her every movement.

"Am I to understand, Mr. Bethune, that miss stops here to-night?" she demanded truculently, and with a very marked emphasis on the "to-night."

Mr. James Bethune got up, and stood with his back to the fire.

"Yes, Mrs. Petticum, she stays to-night, certainly. I hope it is not inconvenient to you?"

Mrs. Petticum slammed down two plates on the dirty cloth in a way which made her opinion on the subject quite clear. Mr. Bethune cast round desperately in his mind for some conciliatory remark and found none.

Judy spoke. "Oh, Mrs. Petticum, don't bang the plates about so much; you'll break them, and they are such pretty ones," she begged earnestly.

Mr. Bethune went first hot, then cold. Mrs. Petticum

would not get over that suggestion for months—being asked not to bang her own plates about, in her own house. But to his utter astonishment it was something else in his niece's address that seemed to have captured the attention of that volcanic personage.

"They are pretty, miss, and uncommon too, for that matter," she remarked almost graciously, and, taking up one of the plates she had just banged down with such force—"My mother had 'em before me, and I've let Mr. Bethune use 'em, he being the quiet, careful sort —till now."

"So am I," Judy assured her. "At least, I'm careful; there was plenty of room to make a noise in at the Orkneys, if one liked. Do let me help you with the supper."

"There ain't no more to it; but you can clear if you like, while I make up your bed," Mrs. Petticum said, and withdrew.

Mr. Bethune breathed a sigh of relief. "My dear child, you must be careful what you say to Mrs. Petticum, especially when she is feeling on edge already," he mentioned nervously. "She took what you said just now in quite surprisingly good part—but she wouldn't do so very often, I'm afraid."

"Well, whatever makes her so short in the temper it isn't cooking," Judy said thoughtfully, surveying the supper. It consisted of (1) a chipped dish, containing three jaggedly-cut, gristly, and rather underdone slices of cold mutton; (2) the heel of a dry loaf; (3) a small piece of cheese that was even drier; (4) a rather smeary jug of cold water.

Mr. James Bethune was conscious of the meagreness of the meal as he never had been before. Generally he read a book over his supper and never gave the food a thought.

"I wonder—whether——? Of course you must be hungry and thirsty after your journey, you poor child! But Mrs. Petticum will be busy preparing you a room, I am afraid," he said hesitatingly.

Judy was looking at the supper with a twinkle in her blue eyes. "Oh, don't bother about me, Uncle Jimmy; I broke the journey, you know, so it wasn't so long. I suppose you generally have cold supper to save trouble?"

"Yes, usually, I think."

"It will never do for Mrs. Petticum to have any extra trouble on my account," Judy said solemnly. "Do you mind waiting a few minutes for your supper, Uncle Jimmy, dear? I know you must be dying to get on with all those nice little Latin exercises."

Mr. Bethune sank into the springless horse-hair chair with a sense of relief. Latin exercises were familiar ground, and a small and active niece who appeared to have never met the maxim "seen and not heard," most emphatically was not. He bent over his corrections, blue pencil in hand, and became absorbed.

Mrs. Petticum was slapping the minimum of blankets on to a small iron bed in the slip of a room across the passage, when she became aware that the door was opening behind her.

"It's me, Judy," that young person mentioned cheerfully. "It's awfully kind of you to make my bed for me; now, can't I do a good turn for you in exchange? Can't I be getting on with the cooking of your supper: what is it to be?"

Mrs. Petticum turned round to stare. "Well, I never! What next?"

"Perhaps you think I can't cook," Judy said. "But I can, quite well. You'll just see. Are you having cold mutton like Uncle Jimmy? You'll see what a stew I'll turn you out—and may I do ours at the same time? It wouldn't cost any more fire."

"It's the gal's night out—there's no one to show you anything," Mrs. Petticum flung at her, in an "That-will-settle-you-miss" tone of voice.

"You bet I'll find everything I want—I'm a Guide," Judy assured her brightly, and disappeared with promptitude. Mrs. Petticum gazed blankly for a second at the door, and then decided to finish the room before going in pursuit and mentioning "sharpish" what she thought of her new lodger's "imperence." It took her nearly twenty minutes to finish the room, however, and by the time she arrived downstairs an extraordinary savoury smell was coming from the kitchen to greet her. Obviously, Mrs. Petticum realised with amazement, this astonishing child was as good as her word, and had a notion of cooking.

The deeply absorbed cook, whom she found swathed in a voluminous apron of her own before the gas stove, did not appear to be wasting anything. The "sippets" of bread, browning nicely at the moment, were evidently taken from that dry heel of loaf; the meat was the meat which had been already cut off, minus its gristle. Judy had discovered for herself potatoes, onions, and a little stock, but Mrs. Petticum was compelled by honesty to own that nothing had been used wastefully, and the stew smelt delicious.

Mrs. Petticum surveyed her new lodger with arms akimbo. "Whoever brought you up, miss, brought you up uncommon handy," she felt impelled to remark.

Judy turned a heated face, which for all its flush wore a most brilliant smile. "I am so glad you think so, Mrs. Petticum, and I hope you'll sometimes let me come and cook again."

Mrs. Petticum, unaccustomedly smiling, did not say no. Mr. Bethune, roused from his Latin exercises a minute later, enjoyed his supper.

CHAPTER III

OVER THE WALL—

JUDY woke early next morning. She was accustomed to doing that, and was usually out and about by 6.30 or 7 at latest, on a fine spring morning such as this.

The little gun-metal watch, which had belonged to father in the War, and had a halo of romance about it, and went sometimes, showed the hour to be just on five-and-twenty past six. "Quite time to get up," said Judy to herself.

She was dressed and out of the house in a quarter of an hour, before Mrs. Petticum or "the gal," not to mention any of the lodgers, had shown the smallest sign of life.

Judy was coatless and hatless, though the morning was distinctly fresh and, so far, sunless; but she hated what she described as the "stuffed up feel" of a lot of clothes.

Not quite a quarter to seven yet, for she knew to a minute how long she took to get up, though she had not looked at Father's watch again. And Uncle Jimmy had mentioned overnight that breakfast was not till 8.30. She had an hour and three-quarters at least in which to explore; time to do quite a lot of sight-seeing. Where should she go? Down to the sea? That was three miles away, so Uncle Jimmy had told her in answer to inquiries last night; one could do it by quick going, but it would leave very little time for doing anything exciting when one got there. It was when she had finally decided against the sea that she thought about the school, over the wall.

Uncle Jimmy had said that he was going to send her there and it would be interesting to see what it looked like before she was plunged into it.

Judy immediately walked round the house and looked up at the separating wall. Rather a high one, but that fact presented no difficulty to Judy Bethune—she had done plenty of climbing. Judy chose her spot with care, and shinned up neatly. Once safely up on the high wall, the getting down on the other side was easy enough. Judy dropped lightly to the ground, and made her way towards the house, taking such cover as trees and rhododendron bushes, more for the fun of it than for any other reason.

It would be a delightful garden for tracking and stalking, she thought, if a little cramped; she hoped St. Oswyth's would turn out to be a Guide School.

She looked up at the house, and an outside iron ladder, coming down to within three or four feet of the wide porch, assured her that fire escapes were properly attended to. That might mean Guides and Fireman's Badge, or it might not. People did seem to get up late in Merchester! It must be seven o'clock now, and no one even shaking a mat at the door. Judy looked at her watch in some exasperation, and discovered that the hands still stood at twenty-five past six. This was evidently one of the days on which the watch had decided not to go!

It occurred to Judy that perhaps it was a good deal earlier than she had thought—the best thing would be to find a clock and discover whether it would be any use waiting for some one to come down and answer her

question about Guides and St. Oswyth's, or whether it
would be more discreet to do the dull thing and go back
to bed.

No clock outside the house, and the windows of all the
ground floor rooms were closely shuttered.

Judy looked up at the first-floor windows. Of course
it would be prying to look into bedroom windows, but
there must be some rooms that were class or music
rooms on that first floor, because the windows were shut.
A bedroom window, of course, would be open.

It would be ever so easy just to scramble up over the
porch, and up the first of those fire-escape ladders, and
have a look in at one or other of the closed windows
which must belong to a sitting-room, and see a clock.
If no one was about, and clearly nobody was, there
could be nobody startled by the sight of a strange girl
on the outside of St. Oswyth's; and if she were seen,
she had only to explain that she was Uncle Jimmy's niece
and a future St. Oswyth's day-girl, merely arriving a
little earlier in the day than was quite usual.

Judy wriggled up the porch and landed herself on the
iron ladder.

But she was disappointed of a clock on the first room
into which she looked, and the next was a bedroom by its
open window. Judy hesitated for a second, wondering
what to do, and heard a clock strike the half-hour, from
somewhere round the corner of the house.

Half-past what? That was the question. The only
possible thing to be done seemed to her just then to go
and see at once.

A stone ledge, about half a foot in width, appeared to
jut out all round the house, marking the level of the
first story, and there was plenty of ivy for a handhold.

Judy took off her leather shoes, and tied them by the laces to the ladder. It was better, with a rather narrow foothold, to have a good grip with one's feet. Then she set out slowly, carefully and very quietly, in search of the clock. And as she came round the corner of the house, she saw some one else who was also taking an early walk on the outside of St. Oswyth's school buildings —a neatly-built, shabbily-dressed man, with a cap pulled low over his eyes, who, unlike herself, seemed interested in the open windows that marked bedrooms. As Judy watched him, fascinated, she saw him put his hand inside a window, open it wider, and prepare to go through the opening made, moving as quietly as a cat. Judy considered him silently for a moment; what was he doing at the windows at an hour when nobody seemed astir?

As soundless as he, Judy withdrew round the corner of the house, and slid in at the first open window to which she came. Quietly as she came, a girl in one of the two little white beds heard her, and she sat up. "What on earth——?" she began.

Judy had a hand over her mouth in a second. "Sh! I'm not a cat burglar, but if you're slick, you'll catch one of the genuines at his games, I think, unless it is not too early for a plumber or a window-cleaner to be getting busy."

Half-unconsciously as she said it, Judy's eyes fell upon a little bedside clock that stood on a little table by the girl's bed. And the clock pointed to five-and-twenty *to* six.

Judy giggled. "That settles it. He's a cat burglar," she cheerfully announced. "Perhaps, as it happened, it's rather lucky that my watch stopped."

She released the girl, who was a jolly-looking person, considerably bigger than herself. "What price telling Miss Salway?"

The girl put on a dressing-gown. The surprise about the burglar seemed to have driven out the lesser surprise of a strange girl walking in at a first-floor window for she asked no questions. "Miss Salways sleeps on this floor," she whispered.

"Go very lightly," Judy continued. "We don't want to let the cat burglar know we're about, too soon."

The owner of the bedroom opened the door very cautiously and peered out. "No one to be seen," she sent back to Judy. "Come!"

There was no sound to be heard either. The burglar was living up to his title very thoroughly, it was plain. "I expect he'll start on the ground floor," the bedroom girl whispered consolingly, "because of the silver."

Judy stopped dead. "You go to Miss Salway, and let her know what's happened. I'll prospect for the burglar and let you know what's happening now." She was off before the other girl could remonstrate.

Judy did not know her way, of course, but she was finding it all right, and finding it very noiselessly. And all the time she was thinking. Where was the silver kept in houses where there was silver to keep? Judy was inclined to plump for the pantry, though, of course, a certain amount would remain in the dining-room.

Judy was at the foot of the stairs when the dining-room door began to open cautiously from the inside. She edged cautiously round by the banisters, and was flattened against the dark part of the great cupboard underneath the staircase, when the cat-burglar crossed the shuttered hall, holding his electric torch to light the way in front of him, and under his arm a bulging bag, the kind of bag in which a workman carries his tools. When he was almost across the hall Judy started to stalk him.

Through baize-doors which did not swing back with a noise, because he held them carefully, and which were just as quiet when Judy followed through them, because she followed his example, as well as his footsteps; down a passage floored with an ugly patterned oilcloth, in at the second door on the right he went. He opened this door very cautiously, decided, apparently, that this was the room he wanted, looked back down the passage, flashing his torch round but mercifully just missing Judy, who had dropped silently to the floor when he turned, and then listened for another second or two with an anxious face. Then he pulled out a chair, after laying down his bag inside the pantry, and propped the door ajar with it. Then he stole past the chair, and he and the light disappeared.

It was very nearly dark in the passage, for the only light came through the shutter to the long passage window; but Judy had made good use of her eyes during the time that the burglar had been depositing his bag and moving out the chair, all with his torch switched on. She was quite sure that the key was not on the outside of the pantry door; of course, it did not follow that it was on the inside, but most doors possess keys.

Judy waited patiently for a whole minute after the burglar had gone inside, though it seemed a horribly long minute, when she expected each moment that some movement from Miss Salway or the girl whom she had roused would scare the burglar and send him bolting with the booty he had secured already.

But there was no sound, and Judy rose to her feet with

the noiselessness taught by much stalking with Guides, and crept to the pantry door.

How lucky it was that the burglar had been afraid to shut the door for fear he should not hear the first sound of rousing in the house! Through the wide chink which the chair held, Judy could command quite a good view of his doings, as he packed silver forks and spoons neatly and quietly into the workman's bag.

Her hand and arm came quietly round the corner of the door: there *was* a key. The question was, could she withdraw it without noise? Judy began upon it and had nearly got it out when the burglar let a fork slip. It went crashing to the floor, and the burglar turned a scared face on his shoulder.

Judy pulled out the key then, with a noisy wrench, and slammed the door to, thrusting in the key upon her side. The burglar was at the door, snatching at the handle with all his strength, just one second late! Judy had the key turned, and she had seen the tiny size of the window. He was a prisoner, unless he had with him tools for forcing locks. Judy bolted back up the passage and through the hall, meeting on the staircase a tall lady in an old-rose dressing-gown.

"Right as rain for the moment," she announced. "Your burglar is locked into your pantry with a collection of your silver in a bag. Phoning the police station, I suppose?"

"Yes," said Miss Salway, "and when that's done, I should like to know who you are?"

"I," Judy assured her, three minutes later, when the police station and the chauffeur's cottage had both been duly notified and other matters could be attended to, "I am a new girl for you; I am from over the wall."

CHAPTER IV

THE GIRLS

ABOUT three hours after she had left the school on that eventful morning, Judy prepared to re-enter it again, this time in a more conventional way.

Between her first visit and her second, there had been a cup of tea made with Miss Salway's own spirit-kettle, in Miss Salway's own private sitting-room, and several biscuits; also a short interview with a burly policeman, who stroked his moustache several times, but remarked in an official voice that if he had noticed her "climbing on the outside of St. Oswyth's at 'auf-past five in the morning he would have felt obliged to ask her business."

Then the burglar was led off, handcuffed and extremely annoyed with life in general, for, as he said, "How could he guess he'd find a blooming kid doing the cat-dodge herself at that time of morning?"

Maura Briarly, excited and wildly thrilled at the idea that a girl who could catch a burglar was really coming to St. Oswyth's, was, with difficulty, driven off to bed, after promising Judy to "watch out for her and show her round." Judy herself was finally despatched by Miss Salways back to Carlton House, with the advice to lie down for at least an hour before attempting to do anything else upon this eventful morning, which had begun so outrageously early.

Miss Salway spoke firmly though very kindly, and she had contrived to point out in manner, though not in so many words, that, well as it had all turned out, she did not approve of girls walking about on the outside of her house at any time of day or for any reason, excepting a fire-alarm with legitimate need for the use of outside ladders. Judy regretfully abandoned a half-formed idea of going down to the sea, now that she had so unexpectedly much time on her hands, and went meekly back to her slip of a room without waking the household.

She only meant to lie down for the prescribed hour, but she went off to sleep, and slept soundly till the " gal," slovenly and depressed-looking, brought her a very small can of lukewarm water and the information that it was "near eight o'clock."

Judy got the breakfast. It was beyond her powers to lay hands upon a clean tablecloth, for Mrs. Petticum had overslept herself and come down in the state of general irritability which oversleeping is apt to produce; but she made the toast, and it was thin, all-crip toast; and she made the tea, and made it with water that was really boiling. Mr. James Bethune made a good breakfast; Judy took care not to imperil his digestion by telling him how she had spent the early hours of the morning, until he had reached his second cup. The story seemed so startling to him that she was sure she had done the right thing in not telling it sooner.

"But I couldn't have known that my watch had stopped again," she said cheerfully, when he began to ruffle up his hair with an agitated "My dear child!"—"and I was going to the school sometime, so what's the odds when!"

Mr. Bethune seemed to find it a little difficult to explain. Mr. Bethune was beginning to realise that the advent of a niece might make life more agitating, but was likely to prevent it from being dull. And Judy cleared the breakfast rapidly, and stacked his exercise-books before he had decided how to clothe the suggestion that people of fourteen don't pay calls on their own, particularly at an hour of the morning when every one else is asleep.

"Five to nine—time we went, Uncle Jimmy dear," Judy informed him, returning with her tweed coat and tam on. "It does seem a pity they don't have a door in that wall; it would save us quite four minutes—for I suppose you wouldn't like to climb over?"

"Certainly not," poor Mr. James Bethune informed her hastily. "It would be a great liberty on my part—and a most unusual proceeding for a classical master. Please don't suggest anything of the kind when you are at St. Oswyth's, Judy."

"You seem rather jumpy about these St. Oswyth's people, Uncle Jimmy, dear," his niece informed him candidly. "I wonder why? Miss Salway seemed all right, and her dressing-gown was topping."

Mr. James Bethune paused on his way down Mrs. Petticum's narrow stairs and looked at her distressfully. "Judy dear, though you saw Miss Salway in—unconventional circumstances, I don't think she would wish those circumstances described in detail to me."

"Well, it *was* a topping dressing-gown," said Judy, unmoved. "Come on, Uncle Jimmy, dear, or we'll be late, and I'm dying to get there and meet the girls who frighten you so."

"They don't—I merely bore them," her uncle told her, and allowed Judy to hurry him round to the back street and through the side gate into St. Oswyth's garden.

"That is the girls' entrance," he pointed out, "but this morning I shall take you to Miss Salway's room."

"Think she'll want to see me again quite so soon?" Judy wanted to know; but school was an unexplored land, and she supposed Uncle Jimmy would know, though it seemed an odd taste in Miss Salway.

St. Oswyth's seemed extraordinarily different now that she saw it with the girls about. Girls seemed to be everywhere, crossing the hall, hustling through a side door, sitting about on hot-water pipes. Judy thought they did rather a lot of staring and whispering, but then she knew she was not used to girls of her own age. They had been very few and far between in the lonely little fishing village in the Orkneys, where she had spent the last six years. She never doubted that they would be friendly and companionable when she came to know them.

Miss Salway was more official and less attractive, in her dark brown tweed coat and skirt, than in the old-rose dressing-gown. However, she greeted Judy quite kindly, told Uncle Jimmy that she would be pleased to receive her as a day girl, and asked her whether she had done any Latin.

"A little," Judy explained. "The minister round our way taught me now and again, when he had time."

Miss Salway looked as though she did not think much of that sort of education, but all she said was: "You are just fourteen, your uncle says; you should be in IV A. You shall take Latin as well as other classes with that form to-day and see how you get on."

"Thank you," said Judy, and then a great bell clanged, and Miss Salway told her "That is for Prayers," and laid a hand on Judy's shoulder and went out with her.

"Say, is that girl whose bedroom I walked into in IV A.?" Judy asked anxiously. Of course, all the girls would be her friends very soon, but it would be pleasant to have one friend to start with, right away.

"No, Maura Briarly is in V A.," Miss Salway said; "and, by the way, Jacobina, I should prefer that your adventure of the morning is *not* talked about to the other girls. I have said the same to Maura. I particularly do not wish silly ideas about burglars to get about —and it would be better that the girls in general should not know that you were——"

"Cat-burgling myself; only for information about the time, nothing else," Judy finished the sentence for her, as she hesitated for a word, blissfully unaware that you do not finish the sentence of Head Mistresses. "Right you are, Miss Salway, and Uncle Jimmy will be awfully relieved that my doings are to be kept dark. He likes a back seat for himself and his belongings too I fancy; he's that kind of man, don't you think?"

"Really, I have not thought of Mr. Bethune at all in that way, I am afraid," Miss Salway said, as they crossed the hall together—a hall now completely emptied of girls.

"I don't fancy that any one has thought of him much in any way," Judy mentioned confidentially, "but now I hope to begin."

She thought that Miss Salway looked at her a little oddly, but she did not make any answer to that remark, but opened a door and with a "Follow me," preceded Judy into a large room with a small dais at one end of it. There was a scuffling sound as sixty-three girls rose to their feet. Judy was face to face with the girls at last!

It wasn't quite such a thrilling moment as she had expected. The girls looked so alike in their navy gym. frocks, white woollen sweaters, and scarlet girdles, that she could not distinguish her friend of the early morning. And nobody that she could see looked the least pleased or the least anything at all, when Miss Salway announced briskly, "Here is a new St. Oswyth's girl, Jacobina Bethune, Mr. Bethune's niece. Stand there, Jacobina."

Miss Salway indicated a chair, and immediately gave out a hymn. Judy stood where she had been told, and wished for the hymn to be over, so that she might begin the process of making friends.

It *was* over; a collect read—the girls rose from their knees, Judy on the tip-top of expectation.

"IV A. will take their Latin lesson here this morning. The remaining forms to their class-rooms."

Miss Salway walked out. Form after form filed out after her in a most orderly manner. Judy was left with Form IV A.—in it but not of it. She stood near the group of girls, wondering when one of them would speak of her.

One spoke, but not to her. "Jolly good cheek of old Dry-dust to plant his belongings on us."

Judy suddenly realised that the speech referred to Uncle Jimmy and herself.

CHAPTER V

THE END OF THE MORNING

THE Latin lesson was purgatorial. Judy no longer wondered that Uncle Jimmy looked tired and harassed. She did the chief part of the answering for the form, despite two or three strenuous nudges from a neighbour, and even an indignant whisper, "You silly ass, no one answers here."

When the lesson was over, and Uncle Jimmy had wearily pointed out the prep. to be done, he went off to the Lower Sixth, and Judy prepared for squalls.

She got them! "Look here, you new girl, what's your name, Jacob something?"

"Jacobina, but I'm called Judy," Judy told them. She wouldn't be silly and mind it, because some of the girls were repeating her unusual name one to another, with an emphasis upon the Jacob, and adding something about a "little Jew."

"Well, *Jacobina*, it's all very well for you to come and swank over the Latin class because you've an uncle to put you up to it——"

"He's been jolly quick if he has, then," Judy said, still trying hard to keep her temper. "I only came last night."

"Why didn't you go to Miss Hemming's School, Emscote?" demanded a rather pretty girl, who seemed to be Erica Finlayson. "None of us think it fair that you should be here, when your uncle——"

"What's that about my uncle?" Judy wanted to know.

"Nothing particular; only we're not accustomed to having relations of the staff planted upon us; you mustn't expect us to like it," was the answer.

Judy had to digest Erica's information as best she could, for V B. and A. were pouring into the hall and swamping IV A. by their greater number. A lesson in physical geography, given by another visiting master, was the next event, and the two forms took it together.

Somewhere in the distance, among the bigger girls, she could see Maura Briarly's bright hair and jolly face, and that was a little cheering. But then, as she remembered a moment later, Maura had been nice to her before she knew about her relationship to Uncle Jimmy, on the staff. Judy had so seldom come up against unfriendliness that she found it difficult to understand. But she did some thinking, which had less to do with physical geography than Miss Salway would have approved, and the result of her thinking was that she would somehow get a word with Maura Briarly when the lesson was over, and find out what she felt about the staff relationship. If her opinion was the same as that of IV A., Judy wasn't going for a minute to hold her to a pledge made in all the excitement of the burglar's capture, and without a notion that she was niece to the classical master. Judy had her own pride.

She got up from her place between two Fourth Form girls, who had seemed unaware of her existence, the very moment that Mr. Warde had finished explaining in what way the configuration of a country affected the characters of the people living in it; and made a bee-line for Maura. The quality which Mrs. Petticum had described last night as "imperence" kept up her courage, and made it possible to put the question as though she did not care two pins about the answer. "I suppose you don't like girls belonging to the staff much, either?"

Maura hesitated for just a fraction of a second before she answered, "Oh, I don't mind, really; you can't help it."

"Thanks awfully," Judy said, her head held as high as it would go, and walked away, disregarding Maura's call to milk and biscuits. Maura meant to be decent to her, Judy acknowledged that, but she had read correctly that hesitation. Maura felt just as the rest did about a girl who belonged to any of the staff, only she remembered this morning, and wouldn't go back on her word.

At one o'clock, as she was on her way to the cloak-room to fetch her coat and tam, Maura ran after her and touched her on the shoulder.

"I say, Jacobina?"

"Hallo!" Judy answered jauntily.

"Care to come out with Nancy and me this afternoon? It's a half-holiday, and we're going down to the sea."

If it had not been for that hesitation in the answering of her question earlier, Judy would have accepted the invitation joyfully. Games and talks and expeditions with girls of her own age had been some of the pleasures to which she had particularly looked forward in the new life, when contemplating it from the Orkneys. But not for her life as things were!

"It's ever so nice of you, Maura, to ask me, but I think I'll be going out with Uncle Jimmy this afternoon," she said cheerfully, and noticed that Maura made no attempt to make her change her mind.

"How did you get on?" Uncle Jimmy asked her, later, when she appeared in the dingy sitting-room, where a lukewarm steak had just been dumped crookedly on the dirty cloth.

"Oh, quite all right, Uncle Jimmy, dear," Judy assured him unconcernedly. "Think Mrs. Petticum would mind if I mixed a little fresh mustard?"

CHAPTER VI

ON THE CLIFFS

"What are you going to do with your half-holiday, Judy?" Mr. Bethune inquired, as the two sat down to the steak.

"It would be topping to go for a walk, if it wouldn't hurt your foot," Judy suggested.

"My foot is good for quite a lot, if it isn't climbing up and down the sort of cliffs you keep in the Orkneys," her uncle told her. "As a matter of fact, if it's cliffs you want, we can get a bus a good bit of the way up to Greenfell Head. Does that appeal?"

"Rather," Judy told him joyfully, and the pair set off together directly lunch was over, to pick up the bus at the end of the road.

"Quite an outing this for me," Uncle Jimmy told his niece, as they boarded the bus.

"Don't you usually go somewhere on a half-holiday?" Judy asked him in her most motherly manner. "You must want the change."

"I suppose it has hardly seemed worth while, as a rule," her uncle said, with a half smile. "Never mind, though; we'll find some nice things to do with ourselves, now you've come, only, I suppose, you'll be off with the girls, once you know them."

"We'll see," was his niece's answer. "I happen to like going out with you."

It was a glorious afternoon, although windy, and as

the bus climbed higher and higher up the cliff road, Judy couldn't help enjoying herself, in spite of the attitude of the girls on the other side of the wall.

Greenfell Head stood out—magnificent, stupendous— against the blue of the April sky; and the glorious green waves were rolling in far below them, each one with its white crest of foam.

"There ought to be good bathing," Judy said.

"There is; and plenty of jolly little sandy coves along the coast."

"Ooh! Can I get up early and bathe?"

"Good gracious, no! Your idea of 'early' is such an elastic one," Uncle Jimmy said, horrified. "You'll have to know about the tides and everything before I let you go bathing, or you'll be getting yourself drowned while the rest of the world are peaceably in bed. It's such a flat shore that the tide comes in precious fast."

The steep winding road came to an end, and there was dry springy turf ahead. Everybody got out of the bus and it turned wheezily in a rather narrow space, picked up about a dozen people who were waiting to go down, and departed.

"What next, Judy?" asked her uncle.

"Would your foot hold out for walking to Greenfell Head?" Judy wanted to know.

Mr. James Bethune was sure that it would, and the two set out very cheerfully along the top of the cliffs, always ascending gradually as they came nearer the headland.

The cliffs here were not terrifically high and majestic, except where Greenfell Head stood up, flinging a defiance, as it were, to the great sea at its feet. In general, Judy thought, the cliffs were climbable in places, at least to within some eighteen or twenty feet of the shore, where the waves at high water had worn them smooth and steep. She lay on an extreme edge to verify the fact, decidedly to her uncle's alarm.

"I won't fall; I'm used to cliffs," Judy explained, with confidence. "Is this cove we're looking into one of the bathing coves you were speaking about, Uncle Jimmy?"

"I imagine it's too far off the town to be a popular resort, so to speak," her uncle told her. "But there's a first-rate cove to the other side of it, with several natural dressing-rooms, which would make it a splendid place for a bathe, if one had time to make a day of it."

"I should love a look at the cave; but the tide is coming in, isn't it?"

"Yes, and I thought you wanted to get on to the Head," her uncle remarked, and Judy scrambled up at last, and the two went on.

Uncle Jimmy was not a very talkative companion; Judy guessed that was because he had been so long alone. She did not in the least mind walking silently while the wind blew, and the gulls wheeled and screamed, and the sea glittered. She marched gaily, two steps to every one of her uncle's long strides, and her hand tucked into the crook of his arm. And so they came to Great Greenfell Head.

Judy stood on the cliff edge looking out seaward, with her tam off and the wind blowing her short curly hair all ways, till Uncle Jimmy laid a firm hand upon her shoulder and pulled her away.

"I suppose you want to do something more in the active line, you slippery young person?"

Judy came back into the present, and the realisation

that Uncle Jimmy had probably walked quite as much as was good for an uncle with a war-damaged ankle.

"If you were to sit down and rest, Uncle Jimmy, and read that book in your pocket, I might do a little exploring quite close, on my own," she said. "I promise you I won't do any falling over cliffs."

"That's a promise," Uncle Jimmy said; he lit his pipe, and subsided on to the grass, in company with a shabby pocket edition of *Lord Jim*. Judy departed with a clear conscience on her exploring expedition.

The row of white-washed coastguard cottages was her objective, and they were only about ten minutes' walk away from Uncle Jimmy's recumbent form. A sweet-faced woman received her very kindly, and answered her eager questions about shipwrecks and rescues, and showed her where the ropes were coiled and how a rocket was thrown. Judy enjoyed it all and did not hurry away, for she thought that the longer Uncle Jimmy lay out on the cliffs in the glorious air, away from Mrs. Petti-cum's dull dingy rooms and the perpetual Latin exercises, the better it would be for him. It was so much the better that when at length she tore herself away from the thrilling stories of the coastguard's wife, and came back to her uncle, it was to find him stretched out on the short, sweet grass fast asleep, with *Lord Jim* on its face by his side.

"Poor Uncle Jimmy, you're tired," Judy said softly, and then she picked up the book and closed it, and set off for a walk in the opposite direction from the coastguard cottages, the direction from which she and Uncle Jimmy had come. Walking fast, she soon came to the lower cliffs above that little cove which Uncle Jimmy had described as so ideal for bathing.

She went and looked down into it again. It would be very nice to explore that cave, but the tide was certainly a very great deal higher than it had been when she and Uncle Jimmy had come past the cove on the way to Greenfell Head an hour ago. Judy remembered what her uncle had said about the pace at which the tide came in on that flat shore, and had just decided that the exploring would have to wait till another time, when something happened. From down below a handkerchief waved.

CHAPTER VII

ADVENTURE

JUDY was on her face, peering over, in less time than it takes to tell it. It had been a handkerchief that waved, she was sure of that, and a handkerchief waving from a cove where the tide was coming in at the double, and the high-water mark was fifteen or twenty feet up the cliff face.

At first when she looked she could distinguish nothing; her eyes seemed drawn irresistibly to the spreading line of white foam, farther and farther up the cove with the breaking of each wave. Then she crept a little farther forward over the cliff edge, and saw two girls crouching under the lee of the cliff, as far away as they could shrink from the advancing waves, caught and cut off by the tide. Judy could not see their faces, but they were school-girls in navy coats and skirts, and one had noticeably bright hair, which the wind was blowing back against the cruel unyielding face of the cliff behind her.

It did not take Judy more than half a minute to make up her mind what must be done and done at once. Above high-water mark the cliff might be climbable; she thought it was—for herself at least—but not the most hopeful person in any world could see a way of getting up that first smooth fifteen or twenty feet. The coast-guard cottages and the ropes always kept ready there were the one hope.

Judy tried to shout a reassuring message, but she was afraid that the wind would have blown her voice away. And stop she dared not, with the tide coming in so fast, and the coastguard cottages so horribly far away. Judy ran like the wind; appeared, panting and dishevelled, before an Uncle Jimmy just beginning to wake up, and fled, after a jerked explanation: " Girls in the cove—cut off"—for the coastguard cottages. Uncle Jimmy, after noting her direction, turned and ran haltingly downwards towards the cliff above the cove, leaving *Lord Jim* derelict on the turf.

Judy shot in upon the friendly woman, almost causing her to drop the kettle she was filling at the tap in the back kitchen.

" Quick! Get a man and a strong rope, please," Judy gasped out, holding to the lintel of the door. " There are two girls down in the cove where the cave is, and the tide . . ."

But it seemed that the coastguard's wife did not need to hear what the tide was doing. Her round, rosy face had turned pale, and her kind blue eyes looked almost circular.

" Dear, dear! and my man and Jack Hissey his mate right on the other side of the Head this afternoon, overhauling the shed of stores," she said. " Cringle's Cove, you said, my dear! Why, there's nothing to hold to, and the sea coming in so rough."

She dived through a back door and called shrilly. " Georgie, run, run as hard as you can, my dear, to Daddy at the shed, and tell him there's young ladies in Cringle's Cove, and he and Jack will need the boat. Run, sonny; 'tis their lives!"

A small boy who had been hugging a fat and obviously

unwilling puppy firmly round the middle, put it down'
nodded, and set off at a steady, purposeful run.

"Now for a rope," urged Judy, who had recovered her
breath while Georgie received his instructions. She had
one of the great coils off its hook in a moment, finding
it heavier than she expected.

"That's right, my dear; a rope end is something for
them to hold to," the coastguard's wife told her, but not
hopefully. "We'll do what we can; but if Georgie runs
his little legs off, bless him! Father can't get the boat
round to Cringle's Cove in less than three-quarters of
an hour."

They were hurrying by now towards the cove. The
woman moving with long strides and the coil of rope
on her arm; Judy running to keep up with her, but
feeling the pace dreadfully slow all the same, when she
remembered how near the spreading line of foam had
been to the two girls pressing back against the cliff in
terror.

"But shan't we pull them up with the rope?" she asked.
"Three-quarters of an hour is a long time."

"I doubt if I'd be strong enough to pull the young
ladies up by myself," the coastguard's wife said; "but
I would try if they knew how to fasten a rope that'll
hold, round themselves. But not one in a thousand can
do that; it needs a man to go down to them. Unless the
rope holds it is sheer murder to try and pull them up
over the cliff face, my dear."

"Oh, that's all right, then," Judy said joyfully. "My
Uncle Jimmy is there to help you pull them up, and I'll
go down and tie the rope for them. I know about knots;
I'm a Guide."

They came together to the cliff above the cove, to find

Mr. Bethune there already, in spite of his lame foot. He was peering down. "I must go to them. They're holding on, but they'll be washed away directly, I'm afraid. Is a boat coming?"

"Not for half an hour, sir," said the woman, and Uncle Jimmy gave vent to a little sound of dismay.

Judy had already taken the rope from the kindly woman. "You must let me be the one to go down, of course," she told him, "because I'm light, and it wants two grown-up people to hold the rope when people are pulled up."

"You, Judy? *No!*" her uncle cried.

But Judy was already securing the rope efficiently about herself. "Uncle Jimmy, it's as easy as falling off a log when you know the knots. I'll see they're all right; but we've got to hurry."

Judy was over the cliff face before anybody had time to say more, the rope trailing behind her like a long snake. The woman caught it, and showed Mr. Bethune how to brace himself and hold his hands, so that the rope would not be pulled away from him. She stationed herself behind him, holding too. Not that there was at present any pull upon the rope, for the small figure in the navy gaberdine frock was scrambling down easily over the climbable part of the cliff face, scrambling with the utmost ease and very fast. The coastguard's wife, still holding the slack rope, came and looked over the edge, then spoke reassuringly to Judy's uncle, who was looking miserable.

"Don't you fear for the little lady, sir; she's got the head and the hands of a born climber, and she's a plucked one. And she and I couldn't have been sure to hold you, sir."

Judy was by now almost at the end of the climbable

cliff; she sent up a shout to the anxious watchers above, and then an "All right" to the even more anxious watchers below, at whom hitherto she had been too much occupied to look. Above, as she zigzagged to find the last bit of foothold and handhold, she could see Uncle Jimmy's thin face and anxious eyes as he lay on the cliff edge, watching her descent and paying out the rope. Below two girls clinging together, pressed against the cliff, knee deep in water already at the breaking of each wave, with scared, white faces lifted to her. Judy recognised the girls now: one was her friend of the early morning, Maura Briarly; the other was the bigger girl called Nancy, who had been behind Maura in the passage when she asked Judy to come with them this afternoon, and was . . . so obviously relieved when she refused the invitation.

That glance up had shown Judy that Uncle Jimmy was prepared for her weight on his hands; the glance down had shown her very plainly that there was not a minute to be lost. She swung loose, and the rope was paid out carefully, too carefully for her impatience, and she swung lower and lower, over the scarped cliff. Down —down—her feet touched water; her feet touched sand; Maura and Nancy were grasping at her hands as though she were miles removed from that undesirable schoolgirl, a relation of the staff.

"Jacobina! You little brick!"

Judy was very practical. "Now then, we've got to hurry, and then we're as right as rain. Who is going first—Maura?"

"Nancy," Maura said, with a little bit of an effort, and Judy was glad somehow that Maura felt like that.

She tied the rope round Nancy rapidly but securely,

showed her how to guard herself from bumping, and warned her not to look down. Then she shrieked, a penetrating shriek, and the rope, with its burden, was pulled upwards to safety, leaving two girls standing in the cold swirling water below.

Judy surveyed the situation critically. "I suppose there's no ledge? If we could get just a foot or two higher—oh, well, never mind if we can't—we're all right My Uncle Jimmy and that nice coastguard woman will pull like Britons, you bet, and there's a boat coming."

"How did you know about us?" Maura asked rather huskily.

"Went for a walk while my uncle was resting, and saw your hankie wave. You stepped out from the cliff to wave it, didn't you? And I was looking for the cave."

"That was what betrayed us; we were exploring it.

"It goes ever so far back, and it was pretty dark, and we didn't know how long we took," Maura continued. "The tide was quite a good way off when we got in. We thought we had plenty of time, but there it was, all splashing up into the cave when we got out—ugh! It was beastly! I think we ought to have tried to round the rocks at the side of the cave before the water got so frightfully deep; but it was so rough, and Nancy thought we couldn't do it—and I dare say we couldn't, for the rocks run out farther than one thinks—and we hoped that some one might pass above and get help from the coastguard."

"Well, some one did, you see, and Uncle Jimmy's jolly strong in the wrists, though he is lame," Judy told her. "Hurray! Nancy is safely up; here comes the rope. Stand ready, Maura; we haven't a lot of time to play round in."

"I'm not going up before you do," Maura said stubbornly. "Why, the water's up to your waist."

"You must; you don't know how to tie the knots, and I do," Judy cried out sharply. "Go on, Maura, don't be an ass. Just hurry, that's all."

The rope hit Judy on the shoulder. She caught it, and secured it round Maura with hands that were almost too numb with cold to tie firmly. She gave her peculiar carrying shriek, cutting into another remonstrance from Maura, and the burdened rope shot upwards. On the top of the cliff they realised her danger, Judy knew; not a second would be wasted, and she must contrive to hold on.

The sun had gone behind a cloud, and the wind was higher, sweeping in waves that seemed unpleasantly big, when you were clinging to a slippery cliff that had nothing on it to cling to, and trying to keep an unsteady foothold on sand that was being sucked from under your feet.

It wasn't pleasant, but it was something to have been Guide enough to know the knots that saved the lives of the two girls. Judy braced herself up, to hold and endure; saying over and over again to herself lines that her father had taught her long ago:

"If you can force your heart and nerve and sinew
    To serve your turn long after they are gone,
And still hold on, when there is nothing in you
    Except the will that says to you, ' Hold on! '"

There wasn't much left now to her, except that will. The braking of the last big wave had brought the cold swirling water breast high for a girl who was small for her age, and had filled her nose and mouth with bitter spray, half-choking her. A monster wave was bearing down upon her now. "*And still hold on.*" She did not know she spoke the words aloud. And a rope struck her head.

She grasped at it, clinging with both hands, while the great wave broke over her, drawing her irresistibly away from the cliff. When the wave had sucked back, she looked up in amazement. Maura could not have reached the top in those few minutes.

She had not. Where the cliff became climbable, according to the ideas of Judy, Maura was crouching beside a clump of sea lavender, to which she seemed to be holding giddily and precariously. It was plain enough that she had slipped Judy's knots so soon as she found any sort of resting place, and sent the rope down to the rescue.

The knots were still there—Judy had only to slip the rope under her arms and draw tight, and that, luckily, was not beyond the power of her numbed fingers. Within five minutes she was safely at Maura's side, well beyond the reach of that tossing hungry sea below.

"You *were* a sport to do that!" she exclaimed, as she knelt down beside Maura, with a steadying hand on her elbow. "It *was* getting a bit uncomfortable down there, when the rope came."

"Did you think I was going to leave you to drown, because we don't know how to tie a Guide knot at St. Oswyth's?" Maura asked rather shakily, and then she let Judy secure the rope round her again in silence.

"I'm going up on my own," Judy mentioned cheerfully, as she started her friend on the last stage of her journey. "A little scrambling will warm me up, and dry my clothes."

As, damp still, but certainly warmer, Judy grasped at her uncle's outstretched hands and was pulled by him over the edge of the cliff, a boat came dashing furiously into the mouth of Cringle's Cove, rowed at the utmost pace of two coastguardsmen's powers. But, for all their efforts, it would have come too late.

CHAPTER VIII

WHAT CAME OF IT

AN agreeable aroma of frying sausages greeted Mrs. Petticum's lodgers as, one very lame and the other very damp, they crept in at her back door.

Mrs. Petticum emerged from the door of the dingy sitting-room as the pair came guiltily upstairs. Her face actually wore a smile.

"Well, there you are at last, Mr. Bethune, and Miss Judy too, and I declare—I'm glad to see you. You're so late, I was frightened something had happened. But you'll be glad to have your tea now, I'll be bound, and I thought you could do with sausages, as children always fancies after a long walk."

She threw the door open with a flourish, and Judy and her uncle gazed astonished upon the preparation for the tea.

A *clean* cloth was on the table, and the cruet shone. A new loaf stood at one corner, and the butter, no longer a shapeless lump, was in a brand-new butter-dish, with a violent coloured china cow forming its lid. The knives and forks had been adequately cleaned and the spoons polished.

"Mrs. Petticum, you dear!" Judy cried.

Mrs. Petticum smiled graciously. "Well, the girl it was put it into my head it was a good drying day, if she washed out some tablecloths, and, well, we thought we might as well have a bit of general clean up, while we was about it. But—bless me, miss——!"

"Yes, I'm wet," Judy stated rapidly; "but I'll be in dry clothes in two twos, Mrs. Petticum, and I'm just ravenous for your lovely tea."

She flew for her bedroom, hearing from it Mrs. Petticum's clicks, and "Dear, dears!" and "Lor, sirs!" as Uncle Jimmy told the story of the afternoon's adventures. It was in an almost respectful tone that Mrs. Petticum spoke, when, five minutes later, she knocked at the door to say, "You leave your wet things on the floor, my dear, and the gal will get 'em and dry 'em. I'm going to make the tea—you should have a hot drink at once to keep off the chill."

Judy and her uncle had just finished the making of a really handsome tea when there was a ring at Mrs. Petticum's front door, and Mrs. Petticum, not quite certain whether to be disapproving or not, announced: "Some young ladies, sir."

Six St. Oswyth's girls walked in, headed by Maura. They seemed to fill the little dingy room. Uncle Jimmy got up, looking rather amused.

Maura spoke. "Please, Mr. Bethune, and Jacobina, we're a deputation from St. Oswyth's. We want, on behalf of the school, to say we're very sorry indeed for having been such beasts to you both. We've passed a resolution to like Latin if we can, and we six are going to Miss Salway to ask if we may start a Guide Company at St. Oswyth's right away—and learn to tie knots and a few other things as well—and have a door made in the wall."

Judy and Uncle Jimmy shook hands with the deputation. "Do come and see Miss Salway about the door in the wall at once," pleaded Maura. "She wants us to bring you both back, if you will."

Judy fetched her uncle's stick. "Topping," she said. "Let's!"

CHAPTER IX

ON THE NOTICE-BOARD

ERICA FINLAYSON bounced into the senior common-room at St. Oswyth's, with only the most perfunctory of knocks. "Is Clare here, please?" she demanded. The "please" sounded as though it were very much of an afterthought; Erica was always inclined to be aggressive and now she was obviously very cross as well.

Mary Coates glanced up from her book. "Hallo, Erica! All on wires as usual? Clare's gone out."

"Where?"

"With that day-girl who was so plucky when Maura and Nancy were cut off by the tide."

"Then it's that Judy Bethune who's at the bottom of it all," Erica said fiercely.

"Come on, Erica, sit down and tell us what Judy has done," Mary suggested pleasantly. "Why shouldn't Clare go out with her, if it comes to that? She seems to be quite a nice kid."

"Since when have we allowed day-girls to dictate what is done at St. Oswyth's?" Erica demanded, with tragic intensity.

"What on earth do you mean?" That came from Mary's friend, Pamela Cole.

"See the notice-board?"

"Oh, you mean Clare's notice about the meeting this evening. Naturally; Clare talked the matter over with the Sixth before she put it up."

"And you agree to it?"

"Why not?" Mary was beginning to be a trifle impatient. "I can't think what you're making such a fuss about, Erica. I suppose Clare can give the rest of St. Oswyth's a chance of considering whether they wish to be Guides or not, without consulting you."

"You know it's not that," Erica told her indignantly. "Anything Clare likes to do but this isn't her idea at all —you know it isn't. It's Judy Bethune's."

"What if it is?" Pamela was tired of the discussion. "She happened to be a Guide before she came here, and of course she's keen to see 'em started at St. Oswyth's—no harm there. Clare and some of us happen to have realised that there is certainly some use in Guides, if Guiding teaches you to do what Judy did the other day. And Miss Salway is willing to let us start a Guide company here, if as many as twenty of us want it. So now you know as much as I do, and you might clear out. We want to read."

Erica did retreat to the door on this very broad hint, but she paused when she got there, and stood looking at the two seniors in silence for a minute. "Look here, is there anything else you want to know?" demanded Pamela, with exasperation.

"No," Erica said quickly, and then, a second later, as though it was shaken out of her against her will. "So Judy has got Clare?"

She went out, slamming the door behind her. "Call her back and make her shut it properly," suggested Pamela. "She's getting a bit above herself, that kid, just because she's safe for her remove and always top of IV A."

"Oh, let it alone!" Mary said. "She doesn't like Clare

doing anything with the day-girl from over the wall. She'll calm down presently."

But Erica Finlayson was a long way off the calming down process, as she flung past the offending notice in the hall and out to the garden. The notice, in Clare's neat handwriting, seemed to glare at her, as though it were triumphing in the score for the day-girl, against whom Erica felt so bitter an antagonism.

And yet, in itself, there was nothing objectionable in it. Clare merely stated that a meeting would be held in the school hall after supper to discuss the question of Guides. But there was only one girl in St. Oswyth's who really knew anything about Guides and that was Judy Bethune, the Latin master's niece, who had arrived so unexpectedly at St. Oswyth's not a week ago, and to whose pluck and resourcefulness all the school knew that Maura and Nancy owed their lives.

Erica had been quite ready to acknowledge that Judy Bethune had shown pluck; but she considered that some of the girls had made quite an absurd fuss about the day-girl; and most of all she resented the notice taken of her by Clare Venning, the head girl.

Erica had fairly worshipped Clare Venning ever since she, Erica, came to St. Oswyth's. Clare had been kind and encouraging, though she could row her adorer on occasions. But she had often allowed Erica to do special work in her study, had praised her keenness and certainly taken more notice of her than anybody else out of her own Form. Erica had gloried in the distinction and enjoyed the envy of the other IV A. girls; but through and above those poorer feelings there ran a very genuine devotion to Clare Venning.

Now Clare had gone with another IV A. girl, and not

even a boarder; she was consulting with another IV A. girl about school things, and school things in which she, Erica, would have no part. If a Guide company were to be started at St. Oswyth's it would be Judy who would be the important person—Judy who would be teaching knots, etc., to Clare Venning and having consultations with her, and so on.

Quite suddenly something seemed to snap inside poor Erica, "I couldn't bear it," she said to herself. "I just couldn't; there shan't be Guides at St. Oswyth's!"

CHAPTER X

UNDERGROUND

It was a half holiday, but one of those doubtful days when the weather seems quite unable to make up its mind what it means to do. In consequence few of the girls had gone far afield; about half a dozen had set out for a shopping walk with Matron, carrying mackintoshes; and Maura Briarly and Nancy Braithwaite had gone to tea at the vicarage, umbrellas being added to the mackintoshes in their case on account of the Sunday hats; but most of the St. Oswyth's girls were playing tennis, or sitting on the veranda looking on. Erica went out and joined these last.

"Hallo, Erica, you're looking glum," Hesba Donne sang out. "Don't you like the idea of being a good little Guide?"

Could any opening be more opportune? Erica leaned against a pillar and called back her answer. "I don't. I've seen too much at home."

"Well, there's a company near us as far as that goes; I always think they look jolly enough," Rose Flenister said.

"Yes, when you see them out on a parade march, or whatever they call it; they've got to—besides I dare say that part isn't so bad," Erica allowed. "But I know the everyday part of it is a frightful fag."

"What do they do?" asked Beryl Sevenake.

"They're always being worried to work up for badges,

for one thing—as if there wasn't enough work to be done already! I know I couldn't get a girl I know at home, Maggie Cottrill, for tennis or anything sensible, because she was mugging up silly badges for her 'first-class' as she called it, all the hols."

That made an impression certainly. "But they don't all worry about badges, do they?" objected Cecily Mill-ward.

"They have to, once they've let themselves in for the business," Erica asserted. "At least, I've never met a Guide who didn't."

"But they go to camp, don't they—and do jolly things like that?" Rose said.

"I should love camping," Cecily thought, and at least half a dozen voices took up her remark. "Rather!" "So should I." "Camping would be topping."

"*We* shouldn't go to camp if we were Guides ever so much," Erica declared. "Look at the fuss Miss Salway always makes about coats if there's an imaginary east wind. She'd say we should catch cold or something. No, all we should get out of it would be having to put in all our spare time over work at those beastly badges, and, when you'd done it, the satisfaction of sewing a little bit of stuff on to your sleeve; and every one telling you, any time you do have any sort of rag, that they're surprised you could do that sort of thing when you're a Guide."

"It certainly doesn't sound much fun," Betty Clarke said. "I shall wait and see what it is like before going in for it here."

"So shall I," agreed several people, quite decidedly, and even Rose and Hesba said: "I shan't go in for it unless Clare is awfully keen; then, of course, I should."

"She isn't," Erica asserted. "She is only calling this meeting to please that new day-girl, Judy Bethune, that Maura Briarly and her special set make such a silly fuss about."

"She was awfully plucky, the way she did that rescue business in the cove," Beryl remarked.

"I'm not saying she wasn't; only I can't see that gives her the right to dictate to us about Guides. Of course, she's keen to have them here because she would be a shining light in them, I suppose, and boss us all."

"What cheek! As though we'd let a day-girl boss us! Clare would be head of the show, of course. Still I'm not keen on Guides," came from all down the veranda, and even the tennis players from the nearest court, who had just finished a set, joined in.

"Clare won't be able to run Guides; she doesn't know anything about them as it happens," Erica said firmly "No, if we start Guides at St. Oswyth's, it means we must submit to being bossed by Judy Bethune."

With which parting shot, Erica walked off, feeling that she had done enough for the present in the way of putting St. Oswyth's off the idea of Guides.

.   .   .   .

The whole school assembled obediently in the school hall after supper.

On Miss Salway's little platform was a small table, with a glass of water—quite impressive that—beside it a chair with Clare Venning sitting in it, and behind her, standing, the day-girl, Judy Bethune, in full Guide uniform, her little trefoil brooch standing out conspicuously, as bright as plate polish and vigorous rubbing could make it, against the background of her blue Guide tie.

The school clapped encouragingly, but the applause was naturally for the head girl. She stood up, and moved a step or two forward to the front of the platform.

"This isn't a formal meeting with speeches," she explained. "I only want to explain to you why I have called it, and then Judy Bethune, who asks me to tell you that she couldn't dream of making a speech, is going to tell us a little of her own personal experience with a Guide company, and to answer any questions about Guides that any one may care to put. . . ."

There was a little murmuring from the rows of chairs; Clare heard it and frowned. "It isn't question time yet," she reminded the school. "You'll be told when it is."

She got silence all right with this remark, and went on.

"I don't pretend to know much about Guides, but it seems to me quite time that we knew a little more about them at St. Oswyth's. To me there is something pretty fine in the idea of making oneself ready to meet emergency when it chances along, whether it is saving life, or kicking a bit of banana skin off the pavement into the gutter and so getting it out of the way of causing injury to any one. We had the chance the other day of seeing what a Guide could do; this evening we shall hear what a Guide can say. I only have to add that Miss Salway is willing we should start Guides at St. Oswyth's, provided that as many as twenty girls wish to join, and Miss Relton, who is coming next week to begin the special cricket coaching, is a Guide already, and is willing to captain us if we are able to start a company. Of course she will only be down here twice a week. Still, I take it that we can do something with that, if we put our backs into the business. Now, Judy—forward please—it is up to our one Girl Guide."

The chairman sat down amid applause which was a good deal less hearty and vigorous than that usually accorded to the popular head girl; Judy Bethune, day-girl, took her place in the fore-front of the platform—a shrimp of a girl, noticeably small for fourteen years.

But she faced the audience with courage, for all her absence of size. Maura Briarly and the rest of the deputation with her gave an encouraging clap, but it was not taken up by the school in general.

"Clare has asked me to tell about Guides, because I've had the luck to be one for three years, and a Brownie for two before that," she explained apologetically. "I'm afraid I shall do it awfully badly, but you can't help wanting other girls to know how gorgeous it is, when you've tried it."

Judy got on to it pluckily enough, after that shy little explanation. She told how Guides came by their name, and what was meant by the Sisterhood into which the new Guide was enrolled, and, to some extent, for what Guiding prepared you. She told about the Guide Law, which every Guide must know before she is enrolled, and about the patrol system and badges, and why one went in for them, and about tracking and stalking and the nearness to the little wild things which Guide woodcraft brings. "It's the greatest game in the world," she concluded; "but behind the game part you know you're doing more than just *saying* ' thank you ' to your country."

Clare led the clapping, which was polite but unenthusiastic, and then led off with a question on her own account.

"If people get tired of it, can they come out?"

"Oh, yes, of course; only then they give up their Guide brooch," Judy explained.

Maura inquired how much a Patrol Leader had to know before she became a Patrol Leader.

Cecily Millward wanted to hear what was meant by a Second Class; but extraordinarily few people seemed to want to know anything, and in the middle of Judy's careful explanation to Kitty Seecombe, Erica Finlayson and several other girls were observed by Clare from her post of vantage, to be slipping quietly out from their seat at the back.

She stood up. "Sorry, Judy," she apologised, and then raised her voice. "Why are you going out?"

"The meeting is over, isn't it?" Erica said.

"No, it isn't; it's question time."

"Need we stay?" Erica inquired. "We don't want to ask any questions."

"Well, at least the whole school is wanted for the voting on the Guide question," Clare said. "We can take the voting now, if so many of you want to go."

Three-quarters of the room had followed Erica's example, to the extent of standing up, though not of walking to the door. Clare had seen that she must hasten matters; all her popularity as head girl would not hold a room, if the girls were in such a hurry to get away.

"I am sure we are all grateful to Judy Bethune for telling us about Guides," she said. "I, for one, feel that I know a great deal more about them than I did, and should certainly like to see Guides started at St. Oswyth's. Will all who agree with me and who would be willing to become Guides, hold up their hands."

She held up her hand. Her example was followed by Maura and the little group around her, and by a couple of girls half-way down the room. Otherwise hands were kept rigidly down.

"Come on! Five—six—eight—only eight; surely more of you are keen on Guides than that," Clare cried. "Remember we must have twenty to start, Miss Salway said."

A slightly sardonic smile appeared upon Erica's face. One more hand wavered, half rose, and went down again.

"Only eight in favour of Guides?" Clare asked again, incredulously, then, as no further hand went up, she added: "The general opinion is against Guides at St. Oswyth's then. The meeting is dismissed."

CHAPTER XI

THE MAN FROM THE LONELY COTTAGE

CLARE walked with Judy as far as the gate; a great condescension on the part of the head girl.

"I can't understand it," she said, disgustedly. "I made so sure we should get twenty, and now I must go and tell Miss Salway that hardly anybody cares, and we must give up the idea."

"Cheek for me to suggest things to you, I know," Judy said; "but couldn't we wait just a day or two? Miss Salway wouldn't be so frightfully surprised if you said it was being considered——"

"No considering will turn eight girls into twenty," Clare remarked heatedly.

"No of course not; but considering might send some of the non-Guide girls to join the eight," Judy told her cheerfully.

Clare stopped and stared at the day-girl. "After the absolute facer we've had I don't feel much like bothering about Guides again," she remarked. "Still, if you're very strong on waiting for a day or two to break the news to Miss Salway, I have no particular objection. It doesn't make much difference anyway. Run along back to your uncle now, Judy, and don't worry over what can't be helped. You spoke splendidly anyway. It wasn't your fault things went wrong."

"Good-bye and thanks awfully," said Judy, and went slowly and thoughtfully out of the gate, and round by

the back road to Mrs. Petticum's lodging-house. The
door in the wall, though promised, was not yet achieved.

Judy knew that her uncle would not be in as yet; she
had told him that she would probably be late, and he
was dining at the vicarage. Judy had visualised herself
busy at St. Oswyth's for at least an hour longer; if the
twenty girls whom Clare had been so sure of getting had
materialised there would have been no end of work to
do, and all such delightful work. Judy had never guessed
that St. Oswyth's would turn down the question of
Guides; she had thought that a good many of the girls
were interested, besides her own special friends, Maura
and Co. She was horribly disappointed; she couldn't
help owning that to herself, though a certain stubborn
pride kept her from showing Clare that she minded.

Judy felt restless and unhappy and hurt; she had never
met unfriendliness in her life, and didn't understand it.
She thought she would try to walk off her disappointment, and then it would be so much easier to have a
bright face ready to welcome Uncle Jimmy when he
limped back from the vicarage.

Judy slipped noiselessly away from the neighbourhood
of Mrs. Petticum's door, and dived down a side street
that was out of sight alike both from the window of
the lodging-house and of the school.

She ran. Judy never walked if she could run, and she
wanted to get away from people as fast as she could.
She put her head down and scudded like a rabbit, and none
of the passers-by recognised the small Girl Guide as she
shot past.

She was not even very clear where she was going.
Her mind was away with her old company, and she saw
again her last parade, the 1st Kirkwall's giving her three

cheers with a will, and her captain pinning the little lone Guide brooch to her tie, and telling her that she would soon belong to a company again, but must carry on as a good " Lone" between.

The company seemed far enough away this evening; Judy wondered whether she had not told the girls the right things to interest them in Guides when she talked from the platform? And yet, Clare, who was head girl and knew everything, had said: "Just tell them what you know about Guiding; they'll like it all," and that was just what she had done.

The girls had been quite nice to her after that affair in the cove, too; Judy thought they had quite forgiven her for being the Latin master's niece, and a day-girl. It was only during the last day or two, when she had been consulting over Guides, that some of them had not seemed to be quite so nice, though she had tried to believe that was only her fancy. Of course Maura and the others, who had come over to Mrs. Petticum's that night of the rescue, were absolutely all right, but some of the others, Erica Finlayson in particular, had certainly seemed rather unfriendly. Judy couldn't understand it all.

However, it was no good being gloomy about it; that was certain; a fresh wind blowing in her face would be the best thing to help her to live up to the eighth Guide Law: "A Guide smiles and sings under all difficulties," Judy felt, and it was probably that idea in her mind that turned her steps unconsciously to the shore.

She had struck a part of it where bathing machines were few, and she went farther in the non-populous direction. Except for a couple of little twin coastguard cottages nestled under the cliff, there was no one living anywhere near this lonely bit of shore.

Judy ran on, though not so fast here, because she had to pick her way among bits of fallen cliff, which had presumably crumbled away with the heavy rains of the earlier spring, which had been an exceptionally wet one. Judy wondered whether it was because the cliff did so much crumbling that the coastguard had abandoned those two little lonely cottages. No coastguard had lived in either for more than twenty years, so Maura had told her, and they were let fitfully, generally to people who were too poor to grumble at the lonely situation, or the lack of ordinary comfort.

Only one of them appeared to be let at present, Judy thought, as she came near enough to distinguish doors and windows in the little old grey stone buildings, tucked away under the towering cliff; at least it was quite certain that smoke was only coming from one chimney, and rather a feeble spurt of smoke at that, was Judy's inward criticism. It was just when she came near enough to the lonely cottage to distinguish the fact about the smoke, that a man burst out of one of the twin doors and began running towards her, running as though for a wager.

Judy had slackened her own headlong pace before this; the tide was too near the high for her to keep to the sand, and shingle is not pleasant for walking on, far less for running. As a matter of fact she had kept as far as possible to the old coastguard path that fringed the shingle and hugged the cliff, though that was so badly kept in these days that it wasn't much easier going there than on the shingle. Judy had thought as she scrambled along it, that if coastguards had still been living in that little huddled pair of cottages, it would not have been allowed that the path should be completely blocked in places by the fallen debris from the cliffs. Two or three times she had been obliged to jump down a foot or so on to the shingle, because she simply could not manage to get past.

The man who came from the lonely cottage had probably known all about the state of the path, for he had made straight for the flatter line of shingle, wave-washed and was splashing and scrambling along it at a great rate, heedless of the soaking of his poor old boots. Judy knew instinctively that he must be in a most desperate hurry, and ran down the shingle to meet him. The hurry probably meant that something was wrong.

Something was very wrong. The man's eyes were wild in his white, unshaved, hollow face. His chest was heaving under his ragged old coat with the pace at which he had run; he cried out, in a queer breaking voice, as he saw Judy making for him.

"Don't stop me—don't you hinder me, miss. I must get the doctor to my baby, that hasn't no mother."

"What is wrong?" Judy asked.

"A fit, and the boy he's lame; I can't send him," cried the poor fellow, and was off again, splashing through surf and scrambling over pebbles, without another word.

Judy thought that his legs would make more pace than hers, and besides he didn't sound as though he had any ideas about what to do for the baby. She ran as fast as she could up the steep slipping shingle to the lonely cottage.

As she ran she noticed, half unconsciously, how little and lonely the twin cottages looked, as they stood there crouched, as it were, under the great frowning cliff. The nearest human habitation must be at least a mile away. No wonder the poor man had looked wild and anxious, if he had to go all that way to fetch the doctor for his sick child and there was no mother to look after things at home.

Judy fairly raced up that last bit of the shingle to the shabby, blistered door, the paintless door belonging to the cottage which had smoke issuing from its chimney. That, of course, must be the cottage from which the poor man had come. And as she ran she went over anxiously in her mind the Guide First Aid that she had learned with the Ambulance Class, though her captain had considered her too young as yet to try for the badge.

The door was only latched; she opened it and ran straight into the kitchen and only living-room of the old coastguard's cottage.

CHAPTER XII

ENTIRELY UNEXPECTED

IT was a terribly comfortless place that kitchen of the former coastguard cottage. The room was low and dark: coming from the clean fresh outdoor world, where there was plenty of daylight still remaining, though it was past eight-thirty, the darkness struck Judy more particularly.

There was a sour stuffy smell, as though very little cleaning, sweeping, or airing had been done for a long time, and the fire in the rusty grate was a small struggling one, half choked with ashes.

But Judy did not realise any of those outside things very clearly just then, for all her thoughts were for the sick baby.

It was lying stiffly in the old washing basket, which evidently served as cradle, the little face discoloured, the eyes staring. A small boy, with a pitiful one-sided look about him, was crouched in a heap on the floor beside the basket, dabbing a wet spotted handkerchief on the baby's head and crying all the time.

Judy flung a glance at the fire; a kettle was on it—that was something, not very hot though; no steam coming from the spout even. She flew at the fire and raked out some of the ashes, giving the fire more of a chance to burn up.

"Quick!" she said cheerfully to the small boy. "Where

do you keep your bath-tub? We must get baby into a hot bath as soon as possible."

The little boy pointed to a sort of button in the dirty wall, which proved, when pulled, to be the handle of a cupboard door. Inside the cupboard was a heterogeneous assortment of household utensils, pushed in anyhow, and piled on one another. To touch the pile seemed rather like to bring down an avalanche; but Judy could not wait to think of trifles like that; she was horribly frightened by the condition of the baby.

The handle of what might be a washing tub was sticking out beyond a dirty ironing blanket, with a pail balanced on top of it; Judy, holding to the pail so that it shouldn't come down, gave a tug to the sticking-out handle.

The tub was hard to move; there must have been something more on top of it than she could see, or else it was wedged. And there wasn't a single second to be lost; she knew that.

She pulled harder, and the tub came towards her, but the whole structure built up inside the cupboard seemed to give way, leaving her the pail in one hand and the tub in the other. There was a crash that seemed to be extraordinarily heavy, even taking into consideration that the cupboard was piled. At another time Judy would have been more puzzled by the loudness of the crash; but her mind was concentrated on getting the poor baby into a hot bath before it was too late. She tugged the washtub clear of the rest, pulled it towards the fire, and poured the hot water into it, testing the temperature with her elbow to make sure that it was not too hot.

Baby, fortunately, was not dressed; she was only wearing a little nightdress that might have been cleaner and an old dirty shawl. Judy had them off in a twinkling and lowered the poor little convulsed figure very gently into the warm water, keeping her arm underneath for support and security.

"There! She is better already," she said joyfully to the little brother, as after a breathless minute of anxiety the tiny limbs began to relax, and the child to breathe. "Poor little darling! I think she is going to do now. Can you push that kettle towards me? We'll have a little more hot water in. Put it so that I can reach it with my left hand, will you? I mustn't let go of her at all, you know—if she is at all frightened she might catch her breath and have a convulsion all over again. Look! She's doing a funny little three-cornered smile; she must be feeling better. Where shall I find a towel to dry her? It ought to be something very soft; she's so wee and so thin."

"Dad, he washed the towel, along of our shirts and baby's bits of things when he came in from the weeding job a kind lady gave him to-day," the little boy said. "They're out on the line; Dad, he was just going to take them in when baby had her fit."

Judy looked doubtfully from her tiny patient to the small lame brother. "Look here! do you think you can get your arm under baby and hold her up as I am doing?" she asked. "Now—very steady—that's right—why,—you're a jolly good nurse—what's your name?"

"Billy, miss," the small boy told her.

"Billy, you're awfully clever. Keep her supported just like that, and splash the warm water over her with the other hand, and I'll get the towel in a moment. You won't move, will you, while I'm gone?"

"No, miss," Billy promised proudly, and Judy dived

out from the dim, stuffy kitchen into the outside world again, that smelt doubly sweet and fresh by contrast.

"Why, how silly of me! I never asked Billy where his father hung the line," she said to herself, and she stood on the edge of the coastguard path, facing the open door, but looking to right and left and upward for the line.

She didn't see it, because she saw something else—something so appalling that for a moment she could not believe the evidence of her own eyes.

Right above the little huddled cottages, the cliff was leaning, moving, slipping down.

To one side of the little grey building lay a fresh heap of debris, a heap that she was sure had not been there when she went in to do what she could for the baby, only a very few minutes ago. In a sudden vivid flash of knowledge, she remembered the extraordinarily loud crash when the things stored in the cupboard fell, and realised what it meant. And now a great deal more of the cliff was falling, full upon the little cottages, and the two helpless children.

Judy could probably have saved herself by a swift dash to right or to left—if it had not been for the children. As it was, she hurled herself in at the open door—to get them out to safety if possible was her one thought.

But she was only half-way across the littered kitchen when the crash came.

A roar like thunder—something that shook the little old stone building to its solid foundations—a crashing and a falling and a darkening all round.

Judy had just time to reach the children and to fling herself above them. Then a heavy weight seemed to descend upon her, and the world grew black.

CHAPTER XIII

AT ST. OSWYTH'S

THE juniors of St. Oswyth's had all been packed off to bed directly the meeting was over; but IV. and IV. A. were Upper School, and stayed up till nine o'clock in the summer term.

It had cleared off into a beautiful evening after the rain, and the girls were all in the garden. Clare Venning and three others were on the hard tennis court, but the grass was still too damp for the other courts to be in use, and the girls in general strolled about in twos and threes, with blazers over their evening frocks.

Erica was the centre of a group from her own form, IV. A. Ordinarily, she would have been watching the match, for Clare Venning's play was decidedly worth seeing, and she had played for St. Oswyth's against the champions from two of the biggest schools in the country, and beaten both. But just now Erica did not feel particularly keen to bring herself under Clare's eye; she told herself that was because Clare had misunderstood her being one of the first to make the move from the meeting. She did not choose to acknowledge even to herself that she was not very proud of the part she had played and did not at all want Clare to know of it.

Erica was not talking Guides at all; she was discussing the prospects of the school cricket, but she could hear echoes of her work from others, as they passed and repassed in their strolls about the garden.

"Suppose we should be struggling with knots now."
"Don't quite see giving up all our free time," and so on.
Erica found herself wishing they would find something
else to talk about now that the matter was all settled and
the school safe from Guides.

It was just half-past eight that a sudden curious sound
broke the evening stillness—a sound that seemed to come
from a distance, and yet was loud—a sound that was
curiously heavy and seemed as though it had crushed out
all other sounds for a whole minute. Erica noticed that
the tennis players had stopped their game for that
minute, and that even Clare, whom nothing was supposed
to startle, looked a little startled then.

After that scared silence in St. Oswyth's garden the
babel of questions and conjecture broke out in full force.
"What was it? How queer! What a tremendous
bang! Sounded like something falling." And then two
of the maids came running out from the kitchen, looking
frightened, and wanted to know if the young ladies had
heard anything.

The maids were quite sure there was something wrong,
and everybody was unhinged and nervous enough to
jump when there came the ordinary homely sound of
a ring at the front door.

Annie, whose business it was to open it, smoothed her
smart afternoon apron and put her cap straight. "There!
There's some one come to tell us," she remarked, though
why a disaster should be reported to St. Oswyth's, Erica
could not see. "It will be a house down, or a fall of cliff
again, or something of that sort you'll see, young ladies
—and there were three men killed and one maimed for
life when the cliff fell in Purdock's Bay, when I was at
school."

The front-door bell rang again. "They needn't be in all that hurry; bad news can wait well enough," Annie mentioned gloomily, and hurried round to the front door to answer the bell.

"Croaker. Annie always is," Erica said impatiently.

Annie was back among them again in half a minute, looking less gloomy but rather fussed.

"Miss Judy Bethune's uncle has called for her, and will she come at once?"

"Judy? She isn't here," two or three voices said.

"She must be—Mr. Bethune says she's never been home. He's been back to see."

"I saw her to the gate; I'm sure she didn't stay here —still, have a look round some of you," Clare ordered, and went round to the front door to speak to Mr. James Bethune, Latin master at St. Oswyth's.

He lifted his hat and limped to meet Clare with a smile. "I say do you mind hurrying that niece of mine. Our landlady is in a bit of a way; she hasn't come in."

Clare explained. Erica, hovering in the offing, heard her explanation.

"She went home earlier than we expected, Mr. Bethune. She and I were disappointed in the result of the meeting —with the exception of eight, the girls voted against Guides, and Judy left the place quite early, I know, for I went with her."

"Odd! I suppose she went for a walk," mused Mr. Bethune, and then as the search party ran up, with the information that there was no sign of Judy Bethune anywhere about the house or garden, he thanked them and said something about going to look for her: "I shall have to row her a bit, I suppose, and point out that this place isn't the Orkneys," he said, and turned to go.

But Miss Salway was coming up behind him; she had been at a meeting at the Town Hall, and must have come out before the end, the girls fancied, because she was not expected home till nine.

Erica and the search party drew back a little in some alarm; Clare was privileged as head girl, but the girls in general were not supposed to be hanging about by the front door. But it seemed as though Miss Salway did not notice for once that they were breaking rules.

"Oh, Mr. Bethune, have you heard?" she asked. "Such dreadful news, phoned through to the Mayor; he gave it out at the meeting, and I really had to come home. There has been a frightful fall of cliff in Purdock's Bay, and those cottages under the cliff are absolutely buried."

"They're not inhabited just now, are they?" Mr. Bethune asked quickly.

"That's the dreadful part—they are—or at least one is. A poor woman died there only last week, the Mayor said. There are two children—one only a baby."

The girls were crowding up to hear, heedless of possible scolding—there was such a throng that the outermost girls reached almost to the gate and attracted the attention of a ragged wild-eyed man who was running down the road. He stopped and, after a second's hesitation, spoke to one of the girls nearest the gate; it happened to be Beryl Sevenake.

"Pardon me, lady, but could you of your kindness tell me of a doctor as 'ud come to my little 'un quick. The doctor as comes to poor folk is out, they says, and won't be in till late, and my baby's powerful bad, and they're saying as there's been a fall of cliff. I must get back—but could you tell me where to find a doctor, quick?"

"Come along to Miss Salway—she'll know," Beryl

suggested sympathetically, and leading the ragged man by the sleeve she made a way for them both through the girls, with a "Let me pass, please! This poor man has a baby ill at home; I must get to Miss Salway about it."

Miss Salway, just beginning to take in the fact that Judy Bethune was missing, did not welcome the interruption at first when Beryl whispered something rather confused about a poor man and his baby; but directly she realised what the trouble was she was kindness itself.

"Don't trouble any more; I'll find a doctor, and come down with him myself to bring some things for baby," she said kindly. "Of course you must hurry back to her at once; you left her alone, you say, with only your little lame boy?"

"No'm; she ain't alone with him; seeing as a young lady she went along to see what she could do for my little 'un—a young lady as is one of them Girl Guides, what was uncommon handy round where I used to live, before I lost my job and come here."

"A Girl Guide"; Erica was not to get away from that term, it seemed.

"That will be Judy; and that's where she is no doubt —looking after the baby," Mr. Bethune said, in a greatly relieved voice. "Where do you live, my man? for I had better come along and collect my niece as soon as she's done all she can for the baby."

The man's answer came as a staggering shock to all who had heard Miss Salway's words spoken only a minute or so back.

"In the old coastguard cottages, sir—the old cottages under the cliff in Purdock's Bay.

CHAPTER XIV

BURIED

JUDY was coming back to a knowledge of what had happened.

Black darkness was all around her; something seemed to be lying across her, pinning her flat. But her hands were in water, and she had the baby held still in one arm, and, oh, joy of joys! she heard the baby give a feeble little cry.

Then she was alive at least. Judy tried to raise herself, and found that something lying across her was fallen plaster, that fell away as she struggled cautiously to her knees. She was stiff and bruised, and dazed; but she did not think that she was really hurt. "Billy!" she said anxiously, as she drew the dripping baby to her knee, wrapping the brief skirt of her Guide tunic round the poor little thing. "Billy, where are you?"

There was a little scuffling movement and then a small sniff. "Please is we all killed dead?" asked Billy's thin little voice.

Judy choked down a lump in her throat that came from the comfort of hearing him speak. She felt inclined to laugh hysterically, but she swallowed hard, and managed to speak steadily.

"Billy, can you move at all—could you get at my Guide tie and undo it? I want to dry baby, and I shan't be able to find anything in the dark."

There was a little scrambling and scuffing close to

83

her, and a sound of breaking plaster. Then Billy's tiny hands were feeling up her; Judy bent towards him, still keeping the baby wrapped in her skirt, and he got the tie unfastened.

"Not at all the right sort of towel, I'm afraid; but it will have to do," Judy said aloud, because there was no doubt about it, talking is a help towards keeping one's courage when the darkness is very dark. "There! She's pretty dry, and she hasn't had another fit, that's something. Hold her, Billy; I've just remembered where that candle is, and I'm going to feel my way over to the shelf and light it. We shan't mind anything when we can see what's happened, shall we?"

"No-o," Billy agreed, rather quaveringly. Judy put the baby very carefully into Billy's arms, as he sat on the floor among the plaster. She couldn't find the little night-dress, but the shawl had been beside the bath-tub, and she had managed to lay her hand upon it in the dark. Wrapped in that, and dried as adequately as could be managed in the pitchy dark, and with only a blue Guide tie to serve as towel, Judy hoped baby would keep warm until she had a light and could discover night-dress and cradle.

It wasn't nearly as easy to find the shelf as she imagined it would be. All kinds of unexpected obstacles seemed strewn about the kitchen, too, and she stumbled against them continually, bruising herself, and twice coming right down on her hands and knees. She fell against the shelf at last, more by good luck than by sense of direction, and it seemed to her hat it was a shelf which slanted oddly, as she had not remembered that it did. But it was the shelf, and the candle was upon it, though it had slipped down to one end and was lying over on its side.

The matches were still in the candlestick, however; Judy thought she had never known before how lovely light could be. And as she held the candle up she heard one of the most beautiful sounds on earth—a little coo of pleasure from the baby. She felt that moment as though nothing really mattered very much, because the baby was alive and better.

Holding her candle on high, she took a survey of the scene, and it was a startling one. Not only the shelf was aslant, the whole kitchen was forced down on one side—the ceiling was atilt, one wall seemed to be absolutely crushed down, and lumps of solid masonry as well as fallen plaster and shattered glass were strewing the floor.

A great beam, half fallen, had wedged itself between the fire-place and wall and, forming a sort of penthouse, had probably saved the lives of all three children.

Outside the shattered window was an impenetrable mass of fallen cliff.

"What has gone and happened, miss?" quavered little Billy.

"A bit of the cliff has fallen over the cottage, Billy," Judy said, "but we ought to be very thankful, for you see it hasn't hurt any of us. We're quite safe."

"But when are we going to get out?" Billy wanted to know.

Judy did not answer the question, as it happened, she couldn't. That was the thing which presumably she must find out; and Judy fancied it would take some finding. She started to prospect, as hopeful as she could.

Judy shook the fragments of plaster out of the old washing-basket which formed the baby's cradle, and put her into her little flannel night-gown, wrapping her again in the shawl above it.

"Now, Billy," she said cheerfully; "you must tell me where everything lives, and we'll all have supper, baby first, of course. Is there some milk about, and has she a bottle?"

Billy directed her, in a far less woe-begone voice. The idea of supper plainly appealed to him, poor little mite! Under his guidance Judy crawled under an ominously tottering doorway into what Billy described as the "back kitchen," a cubby-hole seven feet by four, which appeared to contain larder, store cupboard and sink. At least Judy gathered that from Billy's description, but most of its original purpose was obliterated. Great portions of the cliff had come crashing through, bearing down roof and all in its devasting progress.

The chances of locating anything and making her way to it if found seemed distinctly remote, Judy thought.

It also seemed distinctly dangerous; walls were swaying ominously and ceiling sagging; but the baby at least must have milk. Judy crawled cautiously among the debris and was rewarded. Balanced precariously on a bit of broken kitchen wall that looked as though a touch would send it crashing, was a sort of wire cage, and in it was a jug of milk covered over, half a loaf of bread, and a baby's bottle, that smelt sour and wanted washing.

Judy took these articles out gingerly, one by one, and crawled back to the kitchen proper in triumph. She had noticed a couple of chipped cups hanging to nails on the shelf where she had found the candle and there was a little sauce-pan on the fire. Water was the great shortage, for sign of a tap among the wreckage there was none. Luckily the kettle had been a large one and three-quarters full; a fair amount would be left in it and they must husband their supply. Judy found herself wondering whether she had not been unnecessarily lavish with the bath.

A little water *must* be spared to wash the baby's bottle out; however short of water, you could not let a baby drink out of a dirty bottle. Judy peeped into the kettle to judge the amount of her water supply, cleared a good deal of plaster from the fireplace and pushed in some dry sticks which were in the grate. They blazed up—and in a moment smoke was pouring out into the room, making the already close atmosphere quite unbearable. Judy had quite forgotten that the chimney was probably as completely buried as everything else about the cottage.

Billy was sobbing and choking, and poor Judy had a panic that the baby would have another fit. She flew at the fire, smothering it out with the old rusty shovel. Of course a fire was an impossible luxury just now.

"That wasn't nice, miss; the chimney smokes awful to-night," Billy announced seriously, as though stating news.

"It does," Judy agreed. "Never mind, Billy, the water is still quite warm in the kettle, and we'll give your baby warm milk and water and see whether she will take if from a spoon, as we can't boil her bottle."

Baby was crying now, a weak little cry: Judy had been thankful to hear it through the smoke screen. "But she'll be all right when she's fed," Judy explained to Billy, who nodded wisely, remarking:

"Our baby cries a lot now mammy's dead, but then there ain't no milk 'cept when Dad's got a job."

"If my uncle will let me, and he's ever so kind, I'll bring your baby down some milk every morning before I go to school, that is when we get out of this," Judy added, with a sudden recollection that unknown quantities of fallen cliff lay between herself and that free world where you could go as you pleased, subject to Uncle Jimmy's easy approval.

However, it was no good thinking about that, she told herself. She fed the baby with milk and warm water, and though she didn't seem to approve at first, she was soon sucking down her feed with gurgles of appreciation. To Judy's intense relief she was off to sleep soon after it, one tiny thumb tucked into her mouth.

Then Judy and Billy had their turn; a whole cup of warm bread and milk (and water) for Billy, half a cup only for Judy, for supplies must be husbanded. When the scanty meal was finished Judy made the little boy curl himself up beside the baby in the washing-basket, covered with a bit of her blanket. He was tiny for six years old; Judy could hardly believe it when he told her his age—there was plenty of room.

It was a great comfort to have both her charges peacefully asleep. Judy wanted to do some thinking, and up to date she had been too busy taking care of them. But now there was something to be faced out, and no time to waste in facing it, and thinking what to do. The blocking of the chimney had brought it home to her; when a house was buried as this one was, no air from outside could get in.

Judy knew it was not imagination that the little room was close and that her head felt dull and heavy, so that she wanted to lie down beside her charges and sleep. She found herself looking at the candle with a kind of fascinated horror. It had seemed rather a small piece when she had lifted the candlestick down from the sloping shelf, but it had become terribly much smaller. Before long—dreadfully soon, in fact—it would have

burnt down, and she and Billy and the baby would be
left in that dreadful pitchy blackness which had seemed
so heavy and frightening before she found the shelf
and lit the candle. If there was only something that
could be done before the light went out?

Judy knelt down beside the washing-basket that served
as cradle and said her evening prayers. Then she got up,
feeling better, and looked carefully at the candle, to face,
like a Guide, the length of time she had before the
darkness.

And it was then she saw—something—unbelievable
for a moment, and then certain. *The candle was burning
down upon one side; somewhere there was a draught!* And
a draught meant that they were not utterly closed in;
that somewhere there was a tiny opening to the outer air.

Judy jumped for joy, in the sheer relief of it; they
were a long way from safety yet, and further still from
freedom, but the fear had somehow gone. She picked
up the candle, and went carefully round the dilapidated
walls to find the opening. And at last she found it, above
the shelf where the candle had been. Part of the tottering,
slanting wall had fallen inwards here, and a great mass
of cliff seemed trying to push its way through. A great
mass, but somewhere in it a chink to the outer air.

Judy piled two or three of the fallen stones together
to make herself tall enough to reach the chink; but she
could not dare to do anything to widen it. It would
take so little to bring down the wall. Patience was the
only thing, but patience was easy now. She sat down on
her little pile of fallen stones, and whistled the famous
Guide chant "Found a peanut".

CHAPTER XV

TO THE RESCUE

WHILE a rescue party was being got together with lightning speed under the direction of Mr. Bethune, whose experiences in the War had left him little to learn in the way of digging people out, Miss Salway was putting together brandy, blankets and bandages; Clare Venning waiting upon her quickly and deftly, and also silently, until the sound of a car below sent her flying to the window.

"Oh, Miss Salway, Judy's uncle has brought a car, and there's a dickey-seat behind. Mayn't I go with you? I could help a little," she begged, "and I'm so frightfully fond of Judy."

"Very well," Miss Salway said, after a moment's thought. "I think I can trust you to be really a help, Clare; not an added anxiety by putting yourself into danger by way of trying to help in the work of rescue."

"*Thank you*, Miss Salway," said Clare fervently.

Erica was standing in the hall, white-faced and red-eyed. She heard what Miss Salway said to Clare, for she said it as the two came down the stairs together with the stores, and she stood a little forward.

"Miss Salway, *mayn't* I too?"

"No, my dear, there is no reason to take you," Miss Salway told her decidedly but kindly, for she was touched by the misery in Erica's face. "You are not Judy's friend; if I took any one except Clare it would be Maura, but I'm afraid none of you would be of much practical use. No, go to bed, my dear."

"But I've behaved so badly to her," Erica burst out, beginning to sob a little. "I——"

Miss Salway stopped her. "I can't hear anything now, Erica. If you feel you have not been kind to Judy, I know it makes the anxiety that we all feel doubly hard in your case. But I cannot cumber up the rescuers with useless people. All you girls, with the exception of Clare Venning, are to go to bed as usual."

She got into the little two-seater car, which Mr. James Bethune had borrowed from the vicar, holding the stores upon her knee. Clare scrambled into the dickey-seat behind.

"The rescue party have gone on," Judy's uncle explained. "I can't walk much, you know, and I've an idea that we can get this little car along most of the coastguard path. The vicar is a sport and says he doesn't care what we do with it. There's a chance prospecting might help us to locate the weakest place before the chaps can get there. It's a case of hurrying, you know."

They certainly hurried enough to the sea, but the headlong pace had to modify very considerably on the coastguard path. It was really marvellous, Clare thought, the way in which Mr. Bethune managed to get along on it at all; she found herself forced into a far greater respect for the classical master than she had ever felt before, when she saw how skilfully his long, narrow hands were managing the car along that narrow path with its many obstructions.

But at last he came to a bit too bad for even his powers

of steering. It was just before the path curved round
into Purdock's Bay, and there had been a fall that reached
almost to the edge of the already narrow path. "Is this
it?" Clare asked, awed.

Mr. Bethune smiled a little sadly. "I'm afraid the fall
is a hundred times bigger than this, to judge by the
distance it was heard. But this is enough to block our
way; we must walk now."

He took the roll of blankets from Miss Salway, and
they scrambled round the outskirts of the fall and past
the projection into Purdock's Bay. And here they saw
and realised what had happened.

Above, where the little lonely coastguard cottages
had stood, the cliff showed raw. Below, a great inchoate
mass lay hummocked down to the shingle and half-way
up the cliff; is seemed as though nothing could possibly
be still alive beneath it.

Miss Salway stood stock-still for a moment as she
realised the extent of the disaster, and then put her arm
stiffly into Clare's, as though she felt the need of support.
But Mr. James Bethune went on steadily towards the
land-slide, though with set face and hands that shook
a little.

He scrambled across the outer fragments. "Can you
place the exact position of the cottages?" he asked Clare.
"I've only seen them from above."

Clare stared at the strangely altered formation of the
cliff; it wasn't easy to be quite sure. "There, I think,"
she pointed.

Mr. Bethune did not spare his lame foot, as he scrambled
across the base of the slide in the direction pointed.
Clare followed hard upon him, though. Miss Salway

remained behind, with the stores, waiting till some sort of discovery should have been made.

Mr. Bethune said no word till he had reached the place which Clare had thought had been the site of those ill-fated cottages. He paused and looked upwards.

"Do you think they *can* be alive?" Clare asked despairingly.

"I don't know," said Judy's Uncle Jimmy, and then slowly and with infinite caution he began to climb. "No, don't come after me," he said sharply to the head girl, and, remembering her promise to Miss Salway, she obeyed at once.

Mr. Bethune had stopped, after zig-zagging up quite a little way. With his feet well apart and balanced on two projecting points, he shaped both hands into a trumpet and called "Judy!" There was no answer, only the scrunching of hurrying footsteps on path and shingle, as the men raced to the rescue. Mr. Bethune shifted his position three or four feet to the left, still with the same meticulous care in all his movements. Clare guessed that he was trying to get some clue as to the best and quickest place for the digging out which must be so speedily done if it were to be done in time for these buried victims. He had shifted four times by the time the men were in hailing distance.

"Found anything, sir?" one shouted eagerly.

Mr. Bethune shook his head, and then suddenly dropped down upon his knees, and laid his head to the side. He lifted himself cautiously in a moment, and his tired face had grown suddenly boyish.

"They're all right," he said. "She's whistling like a blackbird. She's whistling ' Found a peanut'."

The men dug and lifted with infinite patience and skill,

and a way was opened in somewhere short of an hour. Judy's voice came out some time before Judy herself could do so, however, and what she said was: "Please tell Billy's father that the baby came out of her fit. One up for the *Child Nurse Badge*!"

CHAPTER XVI

GUIDES

IT was exactly one month and three days later.

The school hall, the same school hall where Judy Bethune had addressed a meeting with all the girls but eight frankly bored, presented an appearance that was strange to St. Oswyth's. For it was filled with girls in the workmanlike blue uniform of the Guides, though still without shoulder knots, or belts, and of course without the Tenderfoot brooch, to be pinned to the Guide tie only when the Guide promise had been made.

It was the morning after the landslide, during break, that another meeting had been called by Clare, with Erica to address it. Judy had been kept in bed by her uncle and Mrs. Petticum, much to her indignation; Judy "couldn't see what there was to make such a fuss about." Perhaps, though, it may have been easier for all parties on this occasion.

Erica was scarlet in the face when she began, but she spoke out bravely.

"I want to say that I didn't play the game about Guides," she said. "I didn't want to have them here, for a reason that Clare knows, but I would rather not mention to anybody else, and I told you a lot of things that weren't true about them to put you off. I am very sorry I did it, and I am going to add my name to the eight who had the sense to want Guides from the first. I am not saying this because Judy Bethune was a heroine last night and saved that baby's life; I'm saying it because Guiding had shown her what to do in the emergency that happened. It wouldn't have been any use in the rest of us wanting to help, because, as Miss Salway said last night when I wanted to go with her, we should have been unable to do anything.

"Judy was a real sport last night—I suppose she would just say she was a Guide; but she saved that baby twice over, by the hot bath and by going back when she saw the cliff falling, to take care of it. I suppose chances like that don't happen often, and it was a mercy this one came to Judy, not to any of the rest of us; but I think we should thankfully accept the chance we have now of getting ready. I am going to put my name down as one of the future Guides of St. Oswyth's, and when Judy comes back I am going to beg her pardon and ask her to begin teaching me my knots."

Erica sat down, still very red. Clare patted her kindly on the shoulder before moving to the front of the platform in her turn.

"I haven't much to add to what Erica has said, except that I think she is quite right to say it. There is no need for me to make any comment on what Guiding enabled Judy to do; you all heard the story of her pluck and sense which Miss Salway told us after prayers this morning. I know it all made us feel uncommonly proud to think that Judy Bethune is a St. Oswyth's girl. But there is one more thing to be said; I did not tell Miss Salway last night as it happened, that, except for eight of us, St. Oswyth's had no use for Guides. What can I tell her to-day?"

There was a perfect pandemonium in reply. It probably shouldn't have been, but it was; and Clare did not seem to disapprove as much as might have been expected.

For every one was shouting " Guides! Guides! Guides!"

.   .   .   .   .   .   -

That had all happened one month and three days ago. It had been a time of fairly hard work for Miss Relton, the Captain, and for Judy; but they had the keenest Tenderfoots to work with, and they certainly did not grudge the time and trouble. And now to-day the Divisional Commissioner was coming to enrol the St. Oswyth's Company.

The seven patrol leaders were Judy, Clare, Maura, and the four seniors of the other girls who had given their vote for Guides at that unfortunate meeting. Miss Relton had suggested Erica, who was one of the hardest working among the Tenderfoots, but Erica wouldn't hear of that. "I couldn't," she said. But she was very pleased when Judy asked her to be a second in the Robins, her patrol.

They chose bird-emblems for all patrols; Robins, Nightingales, Skylarks, Swallows, Blackbirds, Wrens and Thrushes, and very well the little embroidered bird looked, stitched on to the dark blue Guide tunics. The different shoulder knots of their patrol would be pinned on at the same time as the belts were clasped, when the Commissioner gave the word to Judy, "Invest".

The future Guide Company of St. Oswyth's were feeling a shade jumpy, in spite of the assiduous coaching of their one Guide, and agitated whispers reached Judy at the door of the school hall, where she stood listening for the sound of the Commissioner's car to call the future company to attention.

"Judy, do I march up left or right of my P.L.?"

"Judy, do we salute if she asks us anything?"

"Not till you are enrolled—your first salute is given then to the Queen's Colours," Judy reminded them. "Don't get the wind up, you're all right."

There was a sound of a car stopping outside the school. "Sh! It is—no, it isn't—yes, it is—it's the Commissioner," Judy sent back. "Attention!"

There was a stir in the outside hall, the future company stood stiffly, palpitating with nervousness. The one Guide raised her hand to the salute, as the Commissioner walked in, in bravery of silver cords and cockade, followed by Miss Relton in her captain's uniform. After her came Miss Salway, Mr. Bethune, two or three of the staff and Clare Venning's mother; the vicar, the doctor, and last but not least, Billy's father, clean and cheery and not ragged any longer, carrying a Billy who looked as much better as his father did. For Miss Salway and the vicar between them had found a kind motherly widow to take the two little children into her cottage and look after them, and so many people had bothered to find work for their father, that he was doing capitally as a jobbing gardener and went every evening, when his work was done, to see the children. The baby was now as bright and bonny a baby as you could find.

The onlookers placed themselves to one side of the hall; Miss Relton blew her whistle.

"Leaders fall in!"

Crisp and clear the orders rang out.

"Leaders, attention!"

"Leaders, number!"

"To the right to two paces, extend!"

"Company on parade, fall in!"

"Fall out the Queen's Colour party!"

"Into horse-shoe formation, quick march!"

In a huge horse-shoe the St. Oswyth's Tenderfoots faced Commissioner and captain; the Queen's Colours were marched on to the right of the horse-shoe with their escort, Commissioner, Captain and Guide standing at the salute.

The enrolment began. "Clare Venning, forward march!"

"Do you promise on your honour. . . ."

"I promise on my honour. . . ."

The handshake of a comrade, the left handshake of the Guide, when the little trefoil brooch had been pinned to the Guide tie; and then: "Clare Venning, a full member of the Sisterhood of the Guides."

.   .   .   .   .   .

It was over, the last Guide had saluted her Queen's Colours, and had been turned by the Commissioner to face the rest. Miss Relton changed the wording of her "Guides, salute," to the proud "Company, salute!" which now could be said at St. Oswyth's.

.   .   .   .   .   .

The Commissioner stood smiling down at the newly-formed Company, when the Queen's Colours had been marched off, with forty-nine Guides standing at the salute.

Then she spoke.

When she had finished, there was a tiny pause, and then she raised her voice like a trumpet-call. "Patrol-Leader Judy Bethune, forward march!"

Judy scrambled to her feet and marched up, looking startled. The Commissioner held out her hand.

"I have to pass on a handshake of congratulation from the Chief Guide," she said. "Your name has gone up to headquarters for fine service, but what matters is that when the call for service came you did not fail. Guides of St. Oswyth's, I want three of your best cheers for Patrol-Leader Judy Bethune."

They gave them with a will—and a three times three. Judy could only salute dumbly in acknowledgment of something so very unexpected from the school which had cold-shouldered the over-the-wall girl and been bored by the mention of Guides.

CHAPTER XVII

WANTED—A CAMP SITE

Miss Relton, St. Oswyth's Guide captain, made a little pause before she told what she must tell to the expectant Company. She did not like the job.

"Guides, we have to stiffen up under a bad blow and remember the Eighth Law. You all know that when Miss Salway most kindly gave us permission to camp for the last week-end of term it was on the condition that our camp was close at hand. Well, the sad fact is that we simply can't get a possible site. The ordinary camp site is booked right through to the end of September, and the only other available spot in Senning Park is refused to us point-blank by the owner, Sir George Senning. So I am afraid there is nothing for it but to give up our camp for this year and with the best grace that we can. But I am sorry."

Very blank faces greeted Miss Relton's melancholy announcement. Though the St. Oswyth's Guides had been warned that camp sites were often booked ahead for months, and they had not been enrolled till the term was more than half over, they had been hopefully sure that the Captain would manage it somehow. There was a dispirited silence of quite half a minute, while several people felt they ought to say something cheerful and couldn't find it. Then Patrol-Leader Judy Bethune whispered something to Clare Venning and stood forward, small but determined.

"Captain, why won't Sir George let us camp at Senning?"

Miss Relton hesitated again; she did not seem to be quite sure how she should answer that question. Then she smiled.

"Judy, it is not complimentary to us, but we must take it that Sir George hasn't come across Guides. He says he won't have noisy schoolgirls playing at soldiers in his park."

"Oh, what a shame! Horrid old man! Captain, didn't you——?"

"Of course I did, if you mean did I explain to Sir George what we are doing and what we are not. But I am sorry to say that he still refuses the camp site; so, Guides, we must just make the best of it and give up the idea of camp till next year, unless some extraordinary bit of luck comes our way. Get your flags and fall in for signalling."

The Company fell in and did their best, but though the Guide work of the morning was performed with plenty of spirit, there was no denying that everybody felt a a little "down," and no one more so than Patrol-Leader Judy Bethune.

Everybody had been thinking of this camp ever since the great day when the school had gone solid for Guides, and nobody had doubted that there would be a camp; and Judy felt it her fault. Judy it was who had told thrilling stories of camp, so often and so vividly that she had made the very new School Company wildly keen to camp.

Miss Relton dismissed the Company and there was only five minutes in which to change in before school dinner. Nevertheless some indignant Patrol Leaders and Seconds crowded round Judy, who went back to dinner with her uncle.

"The old brute! I say, let's pass a vote of censure on him for the hateful way he talks about Guides, and his meanness about the camp site!"

"Rather! Let's! And send a round-robin telling him what we've done and why," chimed in Erica Finlayson, Judy's Second, who was nothing if not thorough.

Judy grinned. "I vote we wait a bit, anyhow," she said. "Perhaps he mightn't deserve it after all."

She went back over the wall, thinking deeply, and came so quietly into the house next door where her uncle lodged, that Mrs. Petticum, his landlady, looked at her with some suspicion.

Judy and her uncle usually went out together on a Saturday afternoon, and to-day was to be no exception to the rule. Mr. James Bethune looked up from the pile of Latin exercises which he was correcting and reached for a letter on the mantelpiece.

"You wouldn't mind having to wait for me a bit this afternoon, would you, Judy? I've heard from old Kingsbury, who was my batman in the War, and he tells me he has come to live only about seven miles from here with a married sister, and would like a crack over old times. He's very much of a crock and a cripple, I'm afraid, without too many pleasures. I wondered about this afternoon—had you any plans that would upset, old lady? It seems a bit long to leave him till next Saturday, and there's no bus running on Sunday."

"Oh, yes, of course, let's go this afternoon!" Judy cried, with real sympathy. "I hadn't anything fixed up, this will be jolly."

"You won't mind looking after yourself a bit, while

I see the poor chap?" Uncle Jimmy asked, still a shade doubtfully. "There's not very much to see in Senning, excepting for a church with a fine old Norman tower. Sir George won't let anybody into the park, I'm afraid."

"Sir George! Is this the place where Sir George Senning lives?" Judy asked, all alert of a sudden.

"Yes, the village takes its name from his, or he from the village, I'm not sure which," Mr. Bethune told her placidly. "Here is Mrs. Petticum with our lunch tray; we shall have to look alive if we are to get the bus. It leaves the cross-roads at two o'clock sharp, doesn't it? You're sure you're game, and won't be dull while you're waiting about for me at Senning?"

"I promise you I shan't be dull," said Judy with conviction.

CHAPTER XVIII

JUDY PAYS A CALL

THEY caught the bus at the cross-roads, but without too much time to spare; Judy had been nearly five minutes late in coming back to Mrs. Petticum's, and Mrs. Petticum considered unpunctuality her own peculiar privilege. So she was slow in bringing up the pudding, and they had to scramble for the bus to an extent that was not too good for Uncle Jimmy's lame foot and gave Judy no time to change from Guide uniform. However, they caught the bus, which was all that mattered, and were in due course dropped at the point nearest to Senning along the bus route, and set out very cheerfully to walk the last mile.

Presently they found themselves skirting a particularly high and shutting-out sort of a wall, which seemed to be enclosing a truly magnificent park. "That's Sir George Senning's place," Mr. Bethune informed his niece.

"It must be a gorgeous park," was all Judy's answer.

A little farther on, and they were in sight of a village green, very peaceful and old-world, with some picturesque but probably ill-ventilated cottages beside it, and, nearby, the church with the Norman tower.

"That's the cottage!" Mr. Bethune pointed. "I won't suggest your coming in for they are the last word in stuffiness; but you might call for me in an hour, if you will."

"Right you are!" promised Judy, and took a look at her wrist-watch, which happened to be going just then. "In an hour, Uncle Jimmy," she agreed; "and I hope you'll have a nice talk with Corporal Kingsbury."

She stood still and watched her uncle's tall, thin figure limp down the tiny garden path, and disappear inside the door of the cottage. Then, when he was quite out of sight, she walked back rapidly in the direction of Sir George's park. For a great resolve had come to Jacobina Bethune, known as Judy, and Uncle Jimmy had shown her the way to carrying it out by leaving her to her own devices while he paid his visit to ex-Corporal Kingsbury. Judy meant to pay a call upon Sir George Senning, and put the case for the camp site with all the force that she possessed. All that she had heard of Sir George made the idea of the call far from a pleasant one; but she went determinedly none the less, and, skirting the wall Uncle Jimmy had shown her, made her way round to some great gates, with a picturesque lodge to one side of them.

She tried the gates promptly, and found them immovable. Never mind, she must summon up enough assurance to induce the people at the lodge to let her through. She took a long breath and called "Gate!" at the top pitch of a voice which was unexpectedly powerful for her size. A rather flustered-looking woman came running out from the lodge.

"What is it, miss?"

"I'm sorry if I startled you," Judy told her politely; "but would you mind opening the gate?"

"I can't do that, dear," the woman said. "Sir George don't allow nobody in casual-like."

"I'm not casual-like—I'm a caller," Judy assured her earnestly.

"If Sir George was expecting callers he'd have sent down word to us"; the lodge-keeper was firm.

"But callers don't say they're coming; they just come," Judy explained; but the woman still shook her head, although with real regret.

"I'm sorry, miss, but I daren't do it. Sir George is *that* particular——"

"Give him a chance to see if he wouldn't like an un-expected caller for once," Judy pleaded, and a girl of about Judy's own size, who had come out of the lodge door with a half-peeled potato in her hand, gave the woman a little nudge and said: "You let 'er, Mum. She's a Girl Guide—same as I want to be."

"Well, you may try if Sir George will see you, but don't blame me if you're turned from the door," said the woman, and she opened the gate grudgingly, such a very little way that even Judy, very recently fourteen and small for that, could only just squeeze herself through.

However, it was something to have passed that first barrier, and Judy thanked the lodge-keeper politely before setting out to run at her best pace down the long avenue towards the great house. The altercation had wasted a good deal of time when there was only an hour in which to do everything. She mustn't waste any more.

She arrived at the house in rather a breathless condi-tion, and paused for a minute to recover her breath before making an attempt upon the great pull-bell. In that moment that she stood still at the foot of the broad flight of stone steps leading up to the great front door, a shabby bent old man, with his threadbare coat rubbed through at one elbow, came out of a conservatory door, a large tray of seedlings in his two earthly hands.

He started when he saw her, and all but dropped the tray. "Now, now, missy, what are you doing here? Don't you know you're trespassing?" he asked her testily.

Judy spoke reassuringly; probably this old gardener, like the lodge-keeper, was afraid of Sir George.

"Honestly, I'm not a trespasser, or doing any harm at all to Sir George," she said. "I'm just a caller on business."

"Well, I'm blest!" was the reply of the gardener.

"Do you happen to know whether Sir George is at home now?" Judy inquired anxiously.

He chuckled in a rather unpleasant manner at her question.

"I should advise you to ring and find out, missy; and the butler will tell you that Sir George doesn't trouble himself to see children."

"Then I shall tell him to take in my name to his master," Judy replied.

"What is this name you're so determined Sir George shall have, missy?" chuckled the old gardener.

"Jacobina Bethune," Judy told him. "And if you will excuse me, I haven't much time to spare, so I will go along and give it to the butler now."

And, having by this time recovered her breath, she sped up the steps like a lamp lighter, and gave the bell a vigorous pull.

It seemed to ring resoundingly into emptiness. Judy hadn't intended to make so much noise, but the deed was done, and she stood her ground and waited for the butler.

CHAPTER XIX

HER RECEPTION

THE butler was an extraordinarily long time in answering the door. Judy couldn't understand it, for there certainly had been no doubt that the bell had rung. She had expected him to arrive in a great hurry and rather cross with the caller who had rung with such unnecessary vigour, and had her apology ready. But the minutes passed and no one came in answer to her ring. Judy began to feel more than a little bothered.

To ring again seemed such an impossible thing to do, with the echoes of that last tremendous peal still in her ears, and yet the time was slipping away, and she had promised Uncle Jimmy to call for him in an hour's time. She would be obliged to do something soon, unless she gave up the idea of interviewing Sir George altogether, and that Judy did not mean to do, whatever happened. She decided to give the butler another three minutes; she thought he must have had quite five already; and then to ring again.

Her eyes were on her watch, for the three minutes were all but over, when the door opened so suddenly as to take her completely by surprise, after all her waiting and watching, and a butler with a quite expressionless face stood before her.

He did not say anything; Judy had to pull herself together and remember what she had intended to say.

"Good-morning; would Sir George Senning be so very kind as to see me for just five minutes on very important business."

"Sir George is not at home to visitors to-day, miss," the expressionless butler informed her.

Judy was not to be put off by that; probably it was his usual formula. "Will you please take him in my name and inquire, and please say that the business is tremendously important," she said with firmness.

"I do not think it would be any use, miss."

"How can you tell that till you've tried?" Judy flashed out indignantly. "Please take in my name and message —Miss Jacobina Bethune would be very grateful if Sir George would let her see him for five minutes."

"Very good, miss; I will take the message," the expressionless butler conceded. His tone, if it could be said to have any expression at all, certainly implied that he thought it of no earthly use to do as she had asked. "Will you wait in the hall, miss?" he added, and Judy followed him in, rejoicingly, for here was at least another step gained. Sir George would never have the heart to refuse to see her at all when once she had been allowed in.

The hall at Senning Manor was an interesting sort of place to wait in; it was very large, with a lovely polished floor, and a great branched staircase going up from it and ending in a gallery which ran round three sides of the hall.

She walked to the foot of the grand staircase, and thought what exciting things might have happened on it in historic days; she slid a foot along the polished floor, but cautiously because of her stout lace-up Guide shoes, and thought how lovely it would be for dancing on; she peered up the great yawning cavern of the chimney, and wondered whether there were any secret chambers there. And then the butler came back.

"Sir George will see you, miss. Step this way, please."

Judy's heart beat fast with excitement, she was within sight of the goal at last. Sir George was going to see her; surely it would be possible to make him understand how badly the camp site was needed, and how careful the Guides would be not to worry him, if *only* they might have it. She followed the butler, rehearsing speeches in her mind, and filled with high hopes.

The butler brought her through the picture gallery; Judy got a general impression of heavy frames, and men with long curled wigs, or hair tied in queues, and ladies who were shepherdesses or Grecian nymphs. There was no time to look more closely, even if her mind had not all been upon the coming interview on which so much depended.

At the other end of the long picture gallery was a dear little room, which seemed to be a sort of anteroom. It had a tall cupboard, a well-filled bookcase with glass doors, and an old-fashioned chintz-covered sofa and a wonderful view through a long latticed window into the park where the Guides so longed to camp. Judy had just time to realise that before the butler was at the farther door of the little room, and had announced: "Miss Bethune, Sir George," then stood aside to let her pass. The moment had come; Judy walked boldly through the door, and as she did so, heard again that irritating chuckle which she had already heard before that day.

"Come in, Miss Jacobina Bethune," said the cracked mocking voice of the old man whom she had taken for the gardener as she stood before the flight of wide stone steps.

Judy experienced a distinct shock, which was accentuated when she saw the figure seated in a tall high-backed chair, beside a small wood fire. For except for the fact that he had washed his hands, her mocking old gardener, to whom she had been so frank, and Sir George Senning, the owner of this great house and the coveted park, were precisely one and the same.

The surprise deprived poor Judy of speech for the first moment of it. Sir George spoke from his chair, and without attempting to get up or to make her welcome.

"Well, Miss Jacobina Bethune, you wanted to see Sir George, and now you see him, so I hope you're satisfied. I gave my butler his orders so that you could carry out your part of the programme; and since you have now exactly three minutes remaining out of the five for which you asked, you may take a chair and state your business—briefly."

Judy did not sit down. She felt more confident standing up, and she needed all her confidence, for Sir George's dry tone was terribly depressing.

"It is very kind of you to see me," she said, "and I'll get through in the five minutes. I wouldn't have come, only I'm a Guide——"

"I can see that for myself, by the blue garments which I believe you describe as your uniform—only two minutes for your business now, young lady—and your ' uniform,' combined with your ' cheek ' doesn't prepossess me in your favour, I can tell you——"

It wasn't an encouraging reception, but Judy stiffened up her courage by remembering that she wasn't just one rather small girl alone; she stood for the Guides.

"Please, I've come to ask you if you wouldn't think again about that camp site?" she said. "I've just come of myself, you know; it isn't our Captain who has sent me, so if you are angry it must be with me, not her. But if you would only believe that Guides keep their promises like anything, and we would be most tremendously careful to do no damage in your park——"

Sir George interrupted her sharply. "All very fine; but how am I to know that Guides are the wonderful people they seem to think they are?"

"We don't think we're wonderful," Judy told him, "but we do know that we keep our promises. You won't have reason to be sorry, truthfully—if you trust us with the camp site."

Sir George gave vent once more to the chuckle that was so irritating to hear. "You are a very cocksure person for your size," he said; "but words don't go far with me, young lady. You let me see with my own eyes that Guides are some good, and I may consider what you tell me a little more seriously. Good-morning to you."

Judy realised that she was definitely dismissed, and that there was nothing more to do but to say good-bye and go. She had failed; for, of course, Sir George's suggestion was merely a mocking one; how could she hope to show the owner of the un-get-at-able camp site what Guides were?

She said, "Thank you!" with politeness, and went out, trying not to look as dejected as she felt. The butler with the expressionless face showed her out, and the heavy front door shut behind her, with a clang that seemed like the funeral knell of those high hopes with which she had passed through it so short a time ago.

CHAPTER XX

THE POND WITH WATER LILIES

JUDY went soberly along the wide well-kept avenue for the first five minutes after leaving the great house. She was too much disappointed to care to do anything but walk straight on.

Then she began to waken to the consciousness of minor troubles, besides the one big crushing blow. It suddenly began to seem almost unbearable to have to pass the lodge gates again so soon and the people whom she had assured with so much dignity that she was "a caller." They would know well enough that callers are not turned out within ten minutes of their arrival as a rule. They had been doubtful about her before, and now they would probably be sorry for her, or scornful of her, according as they were kind or not, and Judy hated pity almost as much as she hated scorn. Hastily she went over in her mind the lie of the park with regard to the road and Uncle Jimmy's cottage; it would be shorter as well as pleasanter to cut across and scale the high wall that she had noticed, rather than keep straight along the avenue, and pass through the lodge gates. To think a thing with Judy was usually to do it at once; she left the road and plunged into the heavy midsummer luxuriance of the trees forthwith.

It would have been an ideal place for a camp site, she thought. The park sloped upwards to the north, and there was a glorious place dotted with great shady trees, where a clear fern-shaded stream ran down to feed a large shady pond where water-lilies lay floating on the surface of the water.

Judy noticed the break-away of the ground, promising dryness, the running stream, the shelter from north winds, and longed anew for the promise of a camp site. This was probably the side of which Miss Relton had thought; it seemed to Judy, as far as her small experience went, to be nearly perfect. Of course, the stream was probably not drinking water, but that could be got somewhere else, and it would be ideal for washing purposes. The pond, though not stagnant, was weedy, and would not be of much use for practical purposes; though it was very beautiful and peaceful-looking, with its overhanging trees. Judy went down to look at it, and thought it would be a great place for seeing dragon-flies. She knelt down at the water's edge, and looked longingly at the water-lilies.

There *were* dragon-flies skimming among the reeds at the edge of the pond, and darting down to rest upon the water-weeds where they touched the surface. Judy watched, entranced by the vivid flashes of green and silver and blue, forgetful for the moment of her bitter disappointment about the camp site, until she was brought back to earth with a bump by the twofold consciousness—that the tussock of grass on which she knelt was rapidly crumbling into the water and she would go with it if she didn't take care, and also that a noise of angry shouting was coming rapidly nearer, and, with it, the figure of an old man brandishing a stick.

Judy's eyes were keen and she recognised Sir George at once. She stood up, retreated a step or two from the treacherous margin of the pond, and faced him.

"You young thief—stealing my water-lilies," were the first words distinctly audible.

"I'm not a thief, and of course I haven't touched your old lilies," Judy shouted back defiantly. "I was only having a look; any one may look."

"No, they mayn't—not in private property," the old man stormed back, with a wonderful amount of force considering that he was out of breath with the pace at which he was coming. "Get out, you limb, and don't dare trespass in my park again, or I'll set the dogs on you."

"I should love that, dogs are dears to me always," Judy assured him, with obvious sincerity, and beat a retreat in good order.

She reached the boundary wall, made a running jump at it—caught hold and shinned up rapidly, though at the expense of a hole on both knees of her stockings.

The wall was a fine post of vantage; Judy was in no particular hurry to get down. She did not suppose that Uncle Jimmy would be waiting; her interview with Sir George had been so very short. Anyhow, if her sense of direction were anything like correct, she ought to be somewhere near the spot where she had parted with him and, if, as was probable, Sir George had gone back to his house, and were out of hearing, it would be the greatest fun in the world to hail her uncle from the wall, for the sake of seeing him stare round, wondering where on earth the voice could be coming from.

Judy looked down into the peaceful village road, with its thatched cottages irregularly dotted along the green opposite the park wall—and timed her look well, for Uncle Jimmy's tall thin figure, in shabby grey flannels, was just coming out of the door of the cottage where his friend lived, his head bent to avoid a bump from the lintel.

Judy, grinning at the thought of his astonishment, raised her voice in a stentorian shout, "Coo-ee!"

There must have been an echo in the park to add to its many attractions; Judy could have sworn that a faint cry sounded behind her, as though in answer to her own.

But she didn't take any particular notice of it, because she was so enjoying the sight of Uncle Jimmy's mystification, as he looked first down the road towards the little pond, with its picturesque ramshackle bridge, and then up the road along which he and his graceless niece had come an hour ago, trying to find out from where the call came. But he didn't look above, to the top of the park wall, and it is doubtful whether he would have seen Judy had he done so, for a giant beech overhung the wall at that point and she was nearly hidden among its branches.

Judy gave one small ecstatic giggle, and opened her mouth to coo-ee again. But before she had time to utter a sound, the cry that she had taken for an echo was repeated, and it was a cry that had a sound of desperation in it, and certainly could be no echo this time.

Judy didn't waste a second; dropped off the wall so violently that she landed on hands and knees, scrambled up and dashed at a reckless pace for the water-lily pond. For the cry that she had heard was a cry for help, and somehow she felt sure that it came from that beautiful peaceful pond; with its water lilies and water weeds and its crumbling edges that slid down into the water if you knelt upon them.

She was right. It did. Some one was struggling in the pond—a man; Judy did not distinguish more than that fact just then, for the man was deeply sunk among the weeds and lilies, and was only struggling feebly to keep up his head. The water of that pond was deep, Judy guessed; he would drown in a minute if no one came to the rescue.

Judy was thinking hard as she dashed for the margin. To jump in and try to tow the drowning man to shore would be a hopeless business, even had she been far bigger and stronger than she was; she could not get at him without being entangled in the weeds as well.

She measured the distance with her eyes; not very far if she could but get at him. And then she was there.

"Steady on, I'm coming," she shouted reassuringly, unbuckling her belt. If only she had a rope—that belt seemed horribly short, but of course you don't carry ropes about with you on an ordinary walk, and to climb a tree and break off the right length of branch would take too long. The man was horribly low in the water. The weeds must be sucking him down. Judy wondered if he could get a hand up to grasp what she threw him; wondered what she could do if he couldn't. And as she wondered, she was planting herself, kneeling, on the very edge of the pond, and getting a firm grip of a tough-looking root that was pushing its way through grass and sedge.

A little spit of land ran out into the pond at this place; the belt was so much too short that Judy had to creep along it, trusting that it was firmer than the tussock, or the margin a little farther along, which had plainly given way beneath the old man who was now sinking before her eyes.

"All right, I'm coming. Get your hand up if you can," she shouted at him, and, gripping to the root with one hand, flung the belt as near as she could in his direction, with an unspoken prayer, and the feeble hand grasped it.

But her knees were cold and wet; the ground was giving under her. Setting her teeth and gripping for all she was worth to the root on one side and the belt upon the other, Judy backed cautiously.

She pulled steadily on, though the spit was breaking away below her, until the man's head and one shoulder, green with weed, came up above the water. And then it was that she recognised him for Sir George.

"It's—it's you!" she said, and that was really all that she had breath to say, or time either, for as she said it, a great piece more of the spit slid away into the water with a splash, and she only saved herself by a jerk on the root, that brought it more than half away from its moorings. And with that Judy realised that there was no pulling Sir George out; it was merely a question of whether the root would hold long enough for her to keep his head above the water till help came, or whether his weight and the yielding ground would precipitate her into the water first.

Judy gripped the belt more firmly, and shouted with all the breath that she could muster now for help.

It was rather a thin exhausted cry by this time, but it was heard. How Uncle Jimmy got his lame foot over the wall so fast Judy never could imagine afterwards; but he was there suddenly, crashing down the slope towards the pond, and had gripped her arm, just as the root came bodily up.

A long pull and a strong pull from Uncle Jimmy's hands, and Sir George, all duck-weedy, had reached the margin of the pond and was struggling to land. And Judy reclaimed the Guide belt which had done such matchless service. She felt rather sick and shaky now it was all over.

Sir George held out his hand. "You have, I presume, saved my life, young lady."

"It was my Uncle Jimmy who pulled you out," Judy told him.

"I am aware of that, and I am much obliged to your uncle, but I should have drowned before he came but for you. We are all too wet for speeches, and I suggest, if you and your uncle will do me the honour, that we all three instantly adjourn to the house for dry garments and tea. But I should like to say at once, Miss Jacobina Bethune, that I withdraw my doubts as to the capacity of Girl Guides to make good. The camp site is yours!"

CHAPTER XXI

A CAMP SITE THERE WAS

QUITE a crowd of people were standing outside Miss Salway's gate on a certain glorious morning just a fortnight later, wondering audibly at the unexpected sight of a large motor lorry outside the front door. Still more did they wonder when crowds of laughing girls in blue Guide uniform came out to meet it carrying kitbags, bundles of brown blankets, and miscellaneous goods, such as piles of tin plates, and bundles of tin mugs tied together with string by the handles. At least half the baggage had been stored in the lorry, under the direction of Miss Relton, before it dawned upon the onlookers that Miss Salway's girls were actually going to camp, and were in the very highest spirits about the proceeding.

For the camp business had gone ahead "like greased lightning," as Erica Finlayson put it, on Judy's triumphant return from that memorable walk to Senning with her uncle. A thrilled Judy (in a uniform that had been washed, dried and ironed by a sympathetic housemaid, while Judy, dressed in the Sunday clothes of the lodge-keeper's eldest child, poured tea out of a massive silver teapot for Uncle Jimmy and Sir George) had dashed into the hall where the girls were waiting for the supper gong, announcing at the top of her voice, "We've got the site!"

Perhaps it was lucky for every one concerned that Miss Salway was out, and that it was Miss Relton who was taking supper that evening, for the noise that followed was unprecedented in the annals of the school.

The girls cheered, they thumped Judy on the back in token of approval, they besieged her with questions—and supper was three minutes late, because, of course, Miss Relton was as much interested as the girls, though certainly less noisy.

"Sir George was quite a dear, really, though he hadn't seemed so at first," Judy informed them, and the Guide Company might camp in any part of the park that the Camp Adviser and Miss Relton wanted for the site. It was an absolutely perfect spot, and he wanted to be asked to a camp-fire. Why had he changed round so quickly? Judy didn't quite know—thought he understood a bit more about Guides now—oh, and he was pleased because she and Uncle Jimmy helped to pull him out of a pond. Yes, he had fallen in, and if they chose the camp site near the pond he was going to have the sides shored up a bit and fences put to keep the Guides off the weak spots. It was Sir George's car that she and Uncle Jimmy had come home in, and he would send it over the day they came to camp, in order to help out the transport; and would Miss Relton write to the camp adviser this very night, as soon as Miss Salway gave leave?

Miss Relton, at this point, insisted on the dining-room and grace, but Maura Briarly and Erica Finlayson dragged Judy in with them, and provided her each with the third of a chair so that they could go on hearing about it. And Miss Relton, usually so strict about discipline, smiled approval, and joined in the eager questioning as soon as she had served the fish cakes round.

After that, everything seemed to move with astounding speed and smoothness. Of course, Sir George's goodwill, which was extremely definite now he had given it to the Guides, was an amazing help; he sent his car to fetch and return the District Camp Adviser to pass the site, and was so helpful in every way that difficulties disappeared like snow in sunshine.

Good drinking water was procurable from a keeper's cottage near; his gardeners would prepare the site in accordance with the Camp Adviser's directions. There was a whole disused wing of the house in which the Guides could shelter if it rained; his car was altogether at the service of the Captain with a licence, who was prepared to run the camp for Miss Relton, whose licence was still to come.

The Camp Adviser passed the site without objections as to the shortness of the application; Miss Salway had conceded a long week-end just before the end of term exams, on condition that nobody came back ill, and twenty Guides—only a limited quantity were allowed to go—had collected camping kit with enthusiasm, after duly despatching pleading letters to parents for the necessary home permission to camp. And so had come this glorious Friday morning when they were to start for their four days of camp.

Miss Relton was to go with the lorry, but the Captain with a licence, Miss Benbow, picked four Patrol Leaders to go with her in Sir George's car, so as to get forward with the preparations; and Judy, though the smallest as regards size, was chosen as one of the four on account of her camping experience. The car came before the loading up of the lorry was finished, and Miss Benbow hurried the Patrol Leaders into it, remarking that there would be "plenty to do."

They shot off, amid a storm of cheering from the other

Guides swarming over the lorry, and were at the lodge, from which Judy had been so nearly turned away on her first visit, before they had well realised they were off.

Sir George himself met them about half-way down the drive, and shook hands with them all with such a pleasant smile upon his face that Judy wondered she could ever have thought him ill-tempered looking. He directed his chauffeur to turn down a side avenue that would bring them a good deal nearer to the camp site than the place they had intended to leave the car. And so Judy again came in view of the glorious site at which she had looked so longingly only a fortnight back; with the water-lily pond, newly fenced at the weak spots, and the little clear stream rippling along with a delicious cool sound, and folded tents and piles of exciting and rather mysterious camp equipment lying at the foot of the slope.

Judy seized Maura Briarly and executed a wild war dance of sheer delight at the spectacle; the two had to be called to order by Miss Benbow; though in a very kind and sympathetic manner.

Miss Benbow was marking spots for tent pitching, and needed a Guide to drive pegs through the little discs of paper on which she had written I., II., III., etc., or Stores Tent, Wash Place, etc., also the positions where the two sturdy gardeners, waiting her commands, should dig the holes for the camp kitchen, grease pit and incinerator.

Judy was told off to do this, while the other three Patrol Leaders were sent to fetch drinking water from the keeper's cottage to supply the needs of the probably thirsty Guides arriving in the lorry, and also wood from under the trees to get the camp-fire started.

They were all as busy as bees when the lorry announced its approach by the lusty strain of the Girl Guide song, in which every Guide in the lorry appeared to be joining at the full pitch of her voice, to judge by the noise made.

> "We're the Girl Guides marching on the Queen's highway,
>   With a step that is light and a heart that is gay.
>   There is room for me, there is room for you,
>   And there's work in the world for the Guides to do——"

CHAPTER XXII

THE OTHER JACOBINA

THE fine weather lasted right through that glorious camp at Senning; then it broke; two end-of-term matches were scratched on account of weather, and the first day of the summer holidays was hopelessly wet. If it hadn't been—but that's telling too soon.

To begin at the proper beginning, it rained and it rained! It was a day that could not be described as anything but soaking; and Judy felt defrauded. You don't expect it to rain in the first day of the holidays.

She and her Uncle Jimmy had made such gorgeous plans for this first day of the holidays; they were to get right away from Mrs. Petticum's dingy lodging-house rooms, and live out-of-doors by the sea, and bathe from the caves and revel in a picnic luncheon on the sands and only come home when they wanted, and then to the delightful knowledge that neither prep. nor the correcting of Latin exercises would await them.

But you can't picnic when the skies appear to have decided to empty themselves on the earth; and Judy stood by the rain-blurred window of Mrs. Petticum's first-floor sitting-room, trying hard not to look as disappointed as she felt.

"Any sign of clearing?" Uncle Jimmy wanted to know, from the depths of the springless armchair by the empty hearth.

Judy turned round to him. "Not a bit, Uncle Jimmy,

dear. It looks as though it meant to go on and on raining for ever and ever!"

"Hard lines," Mr. James Bethune murmured sympathetically. Perhaps an armchair and a pipe presented certain attractions to an uncle with a lame foot, but he was very sorry for Judy.

"Oh, it's all right," she murmured cheerfully, abandoning the very depressing view through a rain-blurred pane and planting herself cross-legged on the rather ugly hearthrug. "Let's give up the weather as past praying for and light a fire—I'm sure Mrs. Petticum wouldn't mind, if I promise faithfully to do the grate in the morning—and settle down to something else."

"As long as you can square Mrs. Petticum," Uncle Jimmy murmured apprehensively.

Judy laughed. "Mrs. Petticum can't possibly mind what we do when we're going away for three whole weeks to-morrow. Besides, you can't talk by an empty hearth; it's so unsmiling."

Uncle Jimmy watched her in silence for a minute or two while she coaxed the rather heavily-laid fire into a cheerful blaze.

"You're a handy person, Judy; I wonder, now I'm used to you and your ways, how I'm going to get on without you for three whole weeks? Of course, I expect you'll have the jollier time of it with your friend, Maura What's-her-name; but I should like to carry you off to Cragailoch in my pocket."

Judy sat back on her heels and looked up into the thin refined face and kindly grey eyes of the uncle she adored.

"Darling Uncle Jimmy, it's topping of you to say that, and, of course, I would rather be going with you than any one. But you know, even if I'd been asked, it would have been jolly difficult to run to tickets all the way up to the Highlands for two of us; and the clothes are all wrong for a big house. I ought to have a heather tweed properly built! Now, a man always does have tweed suits, and yours looks A.1, now I've sponged and brushed and mended and pressed. . . . No, it's really best as it is.

"In the *Fashionable Intelligence* to-morrow:

"' Mr. James Bethune leaves Mrs. Petticum's lodgings for the Highland Seat of the Earl of Cragailoch. Miss Judy—no—Miss Jacobina Bethune is making a stay of some weeks at the Sussex house of Mr. and Mrs. Briarly, the parents of Maura'."

Uncle Jimmy grinned. "I like your confidential footnote, after the dignity of Miss Jacobina Bethune."

"Uncle Jimmy, do you know how and why I got that weird name?" Judy wanted to know.

"Family name, and rather a famous one at that," her uncle told her.

"Oh, what did she do?"

"Whom do you mean by she?"

"The other Jacobina."

Uncle Jimmy shook out his pipe and got up. "Funny you should ask about her; it crossed my mind only the other day that the bulk of the family papers were put in my charge when we broke up the old home, and that you would probably be rather interested in the record of the famous Jacobina of George the First's day, especially in her diary, which, as far as I remember, has spelling that beats yours to fits. I'll get the box out, if you like; and we'll look up your namesake's lurid record and forget the weather."

The pair of them were in Uncle Jimmy's rather depressing bedroom, with its outlook mainly on a yard, within about three seconds of the finish of Uncle Jimmy's suggestion, but that was because a rather passive Uncle Jimmy was dragged there at Judy's best and most eager pace. And a black tin box, rather battered and shabby, in common with most of Uncle Jimmy's possessions, was dug out and brought back to the sitting-room, and Uncle Jimmy and this modern Jacobina Bethune, in a gym frock, settled down to glean what they might from the family papers of the story of the other Jacobina who lived when George I was king.

And that was the small and ordinary beginning of something that was just as far removed as it well could be from being small or ordinary at all.

.   .   .   .

They opened the black tin box by the fire, now leaping cheerfully in the grate that was better cleaned by Lizzie, the little maid, than in days of old, and took the papers out, and read and dipped luxuriantly.

What Judy liked best of all about the Bethune papers was the little shagreen-covered "Commonplace Book" that had been the property of that earlier Jacobina. The spelling of Mistress Jacobina Wargrave, afterwards Bethune, was distinctly erratic and her composition far from fluent; but she seemed to be possessed of decided views on many matters and to be at no time lacking in the spirit to voice or to act upon them. Judy thought she would have liked her namesake.

But the spirit and self-will which that earlier Jacobina brought with her to the married home, into which she entered on her sixteenth birthday, was responsible for a great disaster to the House of Bethune and for an unpopularity attaching to the name of Jacobina, causing its total disuse among the lady's descendants until a little over fourteen years before the date of this story, when the name had been revived in Judy.

Judy, on her knees by the leaping fire, utilising its light to decipher the faint faded ink and odd phrasing and spelling used by the Jacobina of old, understood at last the history of the long-lost treasure of Bethune.

Hard upon two recipes it began, that history; began with many extra and unexpected capitals but with no stops or spacing, so that it was not very clear where making of the elderflower wine and the removing of grease spots from double pile mulberry velvet left off, and the tragical story of the lost emeralds started. But Judy was nothing if not persevering, and she dug out the story at last.

"Have this day ordered for MYSELFE a new GOWNE, IVORT VELVET and Each Pannier bordered with a SWEET ruchinge of Emerald-Sattin to matche with the Emeralde and Diamonte Necklace and other Family Jewelles of Grate price, the which I am to be Brave in at my lady Ritchling's Assembly . . . Grete care should be taken that the Iron used should not be overhot——"

Judy realised that a portion of the recipe for removing grease spots had strayed from its place, and stirred the fire again to get a better light on the rather complicated search for the treasure story.

It appeared that there had been some argument about the trusting of the sixteen-year-old bride with the complete set of the family jewels.

"Such a fantangle!" the lady mentioned candidly. "One would think Sixteen Years of Age and a Married woman ranked as a mere Baby. But I Stand to My Rights as the Eldest Son's Wife, and my Nails had been at Madam's face I promise, but for the Trouble after to get the Paint out, and that Mr. Bethune will not have me Scratch."

"Madam" presumably referred to some relation who had tried to exercise a restraining influence.

Judy giggled at the comment *re* paint, as she read it aloud to her uncle. "What a terror! And does she mean by her husband Mr. Bethune?"

"Yes; it would have been considered quite improper to call him Charles in those days."

"Let's find why she wants to scratch her relations."

The reason was discovered at length, sandwiched between another recipe and the description of a remarkable comet, "of amazing length and blood-red in Hue, which is held to signify some Grete Disaster nigh at hand."

The "Grete Disaster," given prominence by capitals, had not been far to seek where the House of Bethune was concerned, for the bride, Jacobina Bethune, summarily informed by the "Madam, who will never allow that I do what I desire," that "political differences" forbade her accepting of my lady Ritchling's hospitality, decided in her wilfulness that the refusal was "all Madam's whims and maggots" and that the grand opportunity of airing the Bethune emeralds and the new gown to match them should not be thrown away for "the Old Cat's pleasure." Her young husband was in London, meeting Jacobite agents (but this his young wife did not know till afterwards), who were discovering secretly what support Prince James Francis could count on, did he make the attempt to recover the throne his father lost.

Madam, the obstruction, opportunely took to her bed with a "rheum," and young Madam Jacobina Bethune took French leave and the second-best coach and set forth by herself for my lady Ritchling's Assembly.

If ever wilfulness were over-punished, this was! Some one must have talked—most likely some one at the little village inn where Madam Jacobina met her coach; even she feared to have it drive up to the manor door. The Bethune emeralds were famous throughout the country-side, and the lady was unattended.

The second-best coach was attacked by highwaymen upon the lonely road crossing Ritchling common—a road of ill repute, with the sea on one side—and a wild stretch of desolate country on the other.

The under-coachman, a lad of spirit, and the stableboy who with him had risked dismissal for the young lady's sake, did put up a vigorous resistance; but they were disarmed and overpowered, and the bride was dragged from the coach and robbed of the Bethune heirlooms, for all her strenuous resistance. She was carried into the "Star" at Alfriston, more dead than alive, with her gown a wreck, and her fine spirit broken by the dreadful conse-quences of her wilfulness.

Her commonplace book noted three or four months later the capture of the noted highwayman, "Hare Lambert," so called from his amazing speed in running, "the man Believed to be the Robber of the Emeralds"; but he went to the gallows without confessing, so Jaco-bina stated; "and so my grete Misfortune can never be Atoned."

Poor little wilful bride; she had worse troubles pres-ently to record. Her young husband took part in the rising of 1715, was made prisoner at Preston, and suffered for his complicity on Tower Hill, not a month after the birth of his little son.

"If anything could add to my Trouble," wrote poor Jacobina, "it is the thought that had I not in my wilfulness lost the Emeralds, their grete Value might have raised a Bribe sufficient to have saved my most dear Husbande. . . . All are too generous to reproach me in my Sorrow, but I Bitterly reproach Myself."

The entries ceased abruptly, with the shagreen-covered book not half filled. Judy looked up at her uncle.

"And that's all. Poor little thing! I'm glad they didn't go for her; it must have been quite bad enough without that. I suppose the emeralds were never found?"

"Never; though they would have been very handy at various times in the increasing hard-up-ness of the family, and never more than to-day."

"Whose would they be?"

"Well, mine, I suppose, unless the Crown claimed a bit for salvaged property; I don't know how the law stands, and am hardly likely to need to know," laughed Uncle Jimmy, "but I am head of the family since Hugh was killed at Ypres—not that there is much to be head of in these days! They confiscated the property, you know, for this poor Charles's doings; his baby wasn't allowed to succeed its grandfather."

"Rather rough," Judy thought. "Isn't it queer the way things people did ages ago make a difference to-day? Here are you, living in lodgings and teaching Latin grammar at a girls' school, all because my namesake would go to a party when she shouldn't."

"Not quite—I should be sheep-farming in Australia, or ranching in Canada, or disporting myself as a mounted policeman somewhere in one country or the other, I expect, if it hadn't been for the war and my damaged foot," Uncle Jimmy told her cheerfully.

And that was all that was said about the lost emeralds just then, for Mrs. Petticum bumped the door open with the luncheon-tray, and was so much horrified by the shocking spectacle of a fire in July that it required all Judy's diplomacy and the prospect of her lodgers' departure on the morrow for three weeks to reconcile her to it. Even so the plates went down on the table with a bit of a bang; and Judy and her uncle felt very much as though they were partners in crime with that poor little sinner of long ago, the other Jacobina.

CHAPTER XXIII

A BLOCK ON THE LINE

JUDY's special friend, Maura Briarly, with whom she was to spend the three weeks of Uncle Jimmy's absence in the Highlands, and as much longer as her uncle could spare her, Mr. Briarly had said, was to meet Judy at Charing Cross, escorted by her aunt's invaluable maid, who was to take the two girls across to Victoria and see them into the right train. Judy and Maura were naturally of the opinion that they could have managed this perfectly well for themselves but Maura's aunt thought otherwise. And as Maura had been staying with this aunt, to combine a dentist (unwillingly) with a theatre, she naturally had to accept her aunt's views as to the amount of care needed by girls of fourteen in London. However, she and Judy were to travel down to Dunsterby unescorted, in view of the fact that Maura had come the journey up and down three times a year since she was ten; and that was a great satisfaction to both.

Maura was on the platform, and Judy out of the compartment to meet her, at least a quarter of a minute before the train stopped. An indignant porter said, "them schoolgal terrors!" and the maid behind Maura gasped most realistically; but Judy and Maura didn't care, as they shook hands vigorously and began exchanging news with as much eagerness as though they had been parted for weeks instead of little more than four-and-twenty hours.

"I couldn't have come away before Uncle Jimmy," said Judy. "I did his packing, you know, except the folding of his coats; he does that. Men can fold beautifully, but they always forget the oddments and have to wire for them. What train do we go down by?"

"The 2.35; then we get home to tea. We're to lunch at Victoria; I persuaded Aunt Celia. She wanted us to go to her flat, though she is at a meeting, but a restaurant is heaps more fun, and Prowse will let us choose what we like. Here's Miss Judy, Prowse!"

Judy shook hands, and earned poor Prowse's gratitude by supporting her against Maura, who was sure they had time to pay a visit to the Guide Headquarters in order to get the new number of the Magazine before going to the restaurant for lunch.

"No, Miss Maura, it's all very well to say it's only just round the corner to your Guide place, and you ' won't be two secs.' I know what them restaurants are —and why you couldn't have had your lunch quiet and sensible at the flat passes me, instead of eating dressed-up rubbish in a place where you may have to wait till you're tired before they bring you anything! And I know what my orders are, and they're to be on your platform a good ten minutes before your train goes, and see you into a carriage with a respectable lady of middle age, who is going all the way, and no nonsense about it."

Maura agreed then, good-humouredly enough, and Prowse, victorious, in the taxi, made some sort of explanatory apology.

"I dare say there might have been time for everything; but your aunt not half liking your travelling alone, Miss Maura——"

"I'm not alone—there's Judy here," Maura asserted, with accuracy.

"And such dreadful things seeming to happen on the railway that give you the cold shudders when you read them in the papers——"

"My dear Prowse, it's just the opposite I complain of," Maura teased. "Nothing ever does happen on my railway journeys, except getting there."

A little later on the eventful day the two girls were to remember that speech!

In the meantime, however, they drove very contentedly to Victoria and made an excellent and rather indigestible lunch, with Prowse only mildly remonstrating now and then, and were on the right platform for the 2.35 to Dunsterby, with a good ten minutes in which to find the right compartment.

Prowse walked up and down, seeking it with meticulous care; Judy began to be quite afraid that the train would go before Prowse had satisfied herself as to the fitness of compartment and companions.

"Let's have a look on our own, Maura," she suggested; "or it strikes me we shall get left behind, and have only too much time on our hands for Guide Headquarters."

Maura evidently agreed, and went down the platform in the opposite direction from Prowse at a good smart pace, glancing into every compartment as she did so. Judy kept alongside and looked too.

"Smoker. Smoker. Smoker. I don't mind, but the middle-aged lady might. Only boys in this next one; here's an empty; that won't do for Prowse, though we should like it. There are a lady and gentleman together; she looks a frightfully taking-care sort of person. Can we ask, Judy?"

"Wait for Prowse," Judy suggested. "It sounds a bit odd for us to ask people if they're going to Dunsterby, doesn't it?"

"Take your seats!" a guard called with authority to the people who, like Maura and Judy, were still standing outside the various compartments.

"I say, Prowse is waving to us frantically; she's found the middle-aged one," Judy said.

"Oh, we can't go all that way back; we shall get left behind, and Daddy and Dick are meeting this train," Maura said impatiently. "Come on, Judy, those people are pretty sure to be going to Dunsterby."

An old lady who had come to the window of the next compartment and was buying *The Quiver* from a paper-boy, looked at the two girls and smiled invitingly.

"Are you travelling to Dunsterby, my dears? So am I. Come in here and I will take care of you."

In spite of the suggestion in the last part of the speech the girls couldn't help falling in love with the speaker. She was such a perfect picture of an old lady, dressed in such a delightful old-fashioned way, with a big loose travelling cloak that had a high collar right up to her chin, and a bonnet, actually a bonnet with strings, and beautiful white curls hanging over her cheeks, and quick dark eyes that made a charming contrast. Just the kind of old lady that Prowse and Maura's aunt would approve, Judy was sure, and so was Maura.

"Thanks awfully, we'd love to travel with you," Maura said, and scrambled into the compartment without taking any more notice of Prowse. Judy followed her, and the old lady motioned them to a seat on either side of her, and took a hand of each, beaming upon them. "Delightful! Delightful!" she said, and was still saying

It when Prowse came panting to the window, just behind a rather short man, who looked past the maid into the compartment.

Maura jumped up. "We're all right, Prowse," she called out. "Sorry you had to run, but we're all fixed up here."

The man passed on; Prowse gasped. "That's all right then," quite approvingly; then, as the train began to move, "Good-bye, Miss Maura. Good-bye, Miss Judy."

The train slid quietly away from the platform, and they were safely off at last.

They all settled down most comfortably together. The old lady did not read *The Quiver* she had bought, nor did she talk much. She asked a few questions in her kind way and the two girls did the talking. They told her all about the starting of the Guides this term at school, and the exciting camp that they had and they told how Judy was going to stay with Maura at Dunsterby and why they had been so pleased when their travelling companion spoke to them at the window.

"Though, of course, adventures never happen on a railway journey—at all events not an under-two-hours journey like this," Judy said with regret, and as she said it, everything began.

And the first thing to do anything unusual was the train. It slowed down rather suddenly and jerkily and then stopped dead, without apparent reason or the ghost of a station in sight.

"Somebody's pulled the communication cord," suggested Judy, who had never heard of the thing being actually done and felt it would be an interesting experience.

The old lady with the white curls said nothing at all; she seemed a little nervous.

They waited ten minutes, the two girls with their heads well out of the window, and the old lady well back in her seat, beginning to take a belated interest in *The Quiver*, perhaps for the calming of her nerves. Then a guard came swinging himself along the stationary train on the footboard—dignified and reassuring.

"Nothing to be alarmed about, ladies and gentlemen. There has been a slight haccident, but with 'appily no injury to life nor limb. The train in front of us has derailed at the curve, we are informed, tearing up a bit of the permanent way; and till the breakdown gang can get to it, there's a block on the line."

CHAPTER XXIV

A GENTLE STROLL

"WHAT a swiz!" Maura cried out, and then she stopped grumbling, for after all the thing couldn't be helped.

"We'll be fearfully late at Dunsterby, I expect; we ought to let your people know, of course—only, how can we?" Judy contributed.

"Don't know. Wonder where we are?" Maura stared thoughtfully from the window. "I *think* we're crossing Ritchling Common; there's a bad curve somewhere near the end of it, to avoid the wide bit of the tidal river, that's probably where the train derailed. I wish it had happened nearer a town; we could have wired, and Daddy might have sent the car."

"Isn't Ritchling Common near anything?" Judy asked. She had a vague sense as she spoke the name of having heard it before, but her mind was far too much on the important subject of how to get on to wonder where or in what connection.

"Miles from anywhere, I'm afraid, except the sea." Maura was discouraging. Judy looked from the window to the far corner, where the old lady was glancing up from *The Quiver*.

"Let's ask her what she thinks."

They went and stood opposite the old lady and inquired her opinion. Maura had an idea that there was a village somewhere not too far away, thought, but couldn't be quite sure, as she and Daddy had come through it motoring. If it were the one she had seen, she was certain there was a confectioner's and a post office.

"What did you say was the name of the village, my dear?" the old lady asked.

Maura hadn't said, for the good reason that she didn't know. "But it was an awfully pretty little place, I know, with an old windmill above it."

"Let's ask the guard how long he thinks we shall have to wait here," suggested Judy. "If it's long, and I should think it would be, couldn't we have a stroll along as far as a signpost anyway. You're sure to remember the name of your village if you see it on a signpost, Maura."

Maura quite approved this idea, but the guard seemed to have completely disappeared again, and the old lady disapproved of calling, in the hope of bringing him along. She seemed also to like the idea of getting out to do a little exploration and seemed anxious to do it quickly, while the guard was not at hand to see them do it.

"It is, I believe, a habit with guards to disapprove of people getting out of trains excepting at a station," she remarked. "But you are quite right to think of the anxiety of your parents, my dears. I will come with you, and together we will take a gentle little stroll in search of the post office situated in the village with a windmill above it."

Since the old lady was so sportingly inclined, any faint doubts which Judy and Maura might have felt as to the propriety of leaving the train vanished at once.

The chief difficulty that occurred to Judy was how in the world to get the type of old lady who wore a bonnet to manage the very long drop between the step and the ground. Until that moment Judy had not realised how much difference a platform made.

She drew Maura to the window and pointed out the depth of the drop in an undertone, her back to the old lady to make sure she didn't hear.

"You get out first, won't you, Maura; you're a bit bigger than I am; you help her from below and I'll hang on above. And, I say, Maura, look the other way while she's getting down; that kind of old lady minds awfully if any one sees above the tops of her elastic-sided boots, you know."

Maura smiled. "Right-o, Judy; it's brainy of you to remember that. I'll keep my head round."

She dropped neatly to the ground. "It's as easy as easy—come on!"

"Maura is down; she'll help you, and I'll hold on above, you know," Judy encouraged the old lady.

Now it came to the point, she seemed distinctly nervous. "Pray look out first, my dear, to ascertain that neither the guard—nor any member of the other sex is about," she entreated. "I should not like——"

"Quite clear," encouraged Judy, after a rapid glance up and down. "The only men about have got their backs to us; I think they're going to look at the damage."

The old lady on that got down with a wonderful agility. Maura, head studiously turned away, received her carefully, but really Judy thought that more gymnastics than she had imagined had been taught in the old lady's youth.

She followed the other two with great celerity, and the three stood at the side of the line looking at the train which seemed to tower so unusually high above them.

But the old lady, at all events, was not disposed to

loiter. She picked up her voluminous skirts at both sides in a very purposeful manner. "Come, my dears!"

The three set off across the common, Maura in front, trying to remember landmarks and sight the windmill, which seemed to be the only one of which she was quite clear, and Judy, walking with the old lady, whose skirts were certainly not at all adapted for a cross-country walk, and who seemed to feel their inconvenience more than the girls would have expected. However, she certainly was what both girls described inwardly as "a sport"; and was quite determined to make her way somehow to the village of the post office and windmill, and even refused Judy's polite suggestions, made at intervals, of pausing for rest.

After nearly a mile of roughish walking, from the point of view of a wearer of long skirts and elastic-sided boots, the fellow-travellers were rewarded by striking a road, and only a few yards along it, cross-roads and a signpost with long pointing arms.

Judy and Maura left the old lady for the moment and made a simultaneous rush for it.

"Frisby three and three-quarter miles. Ritchling four miles. Hurstling six and a quarter miles, Lulliston one and a half miles," they chanted in chorus, and at the last name Maura broke into a squeal of ecstasy.

"That's it!—that's the place with the post office; I remember it now. And it's only a mile away; well another half doesn't count really, does it? It won't take us any time; we ought to see the windmill directly."

It was true; the windmill was sighted in a very few minutes, though the getting to it was a longer business than it looked. Still, there could be no denying the fact that this old lady tramped along most gallantly and that her idea of a "gentle stroll" seemed to be what more ordinary people would have described as a "sharp walk." The windmill was quite near before she slackened her pace or showed the slightest sign of being tired, and then quite suddenly she seemed to crumple. Her pace became slower, and she stumbled twice; then held her hand to the region where Girl Guides knew the heart to live.

"My dears, I don't feel very well," she said pathetically. "I think it would be wiser for me to sit down in the shade of this windmill, while you go on to find the post office and send your wire."

Judy and Maura looked at one another in some self-reproach. They felt that they had been to blame; probably they ought to have seen that the old lady was getting tired before she mentioned it.

Maura helped her to a seat in a patch of shadow; Judy provided her coat as a cushion. Then they looked anxiously at their companion, and observed with relief that she had not changed colour or done anything alarming, as far as appearances went. "But I don't think we should like to leave you, when you're feeling ill," Judy murmured apologetically.

The unselfish old lady, however, would not hear for one moment of allowing the girls to remain with her; they must find the post office at once, she assured them, and put their people out of their anxiety. If she felt better, she would stroll on to the village to find them, but she was not quite sure she should not return to the train and rest there, so they must not be alarmed if they did not find her.

Neither Maura nor Judy felt quite satisfied with this arrangement; it didn't seemed at all the right thing to leave an overtired old lady sitting by herself under the shade of a half-ruinous old windmill. "Suppose she had a heart attack, or something awful like that?" Judy mentioned to Maura in the lowest of whispers, but it was certainly a little difficult to think of staying when they had been told so decidedly to go on. Besides, Maura's people would be so dreadfully anxious if they didn't send a wire!

Finally they said a rather doubtful good-bye to the old lady and went off in search of the post office, after promising faithfully to be as quick as possible.

They looked back once when they had gone a little way and waved; but the old lady did not see them. She was evidently feeling much more rested, for she was standing up, her face towards the windmill. She seemed to find it interesting.

CHAPTER XXV

THE CHURCHYARD AT LULLISTON

You can walk a mile and a half at a good round pace when you choose. Judy and Maura did choose, for they did not feel quite happy about the old lady left behind at the windmill.

The ground began to slope rather rapidly soon after they left it behind, and Maura presently recognised a steep and stony hill, which her father had said wanted "negotiating" with a car of which the brakes were not in perfect condition.

"I shouldn't think they've mended the road for the last couple of hundred years," Maura suggested, as they picked their way among the loose stones, and something stirred vaguely at the back of Judy's mind; something that was perhaps roused by Maura's date, palpable exaggeration though it was. "I wonder if we shall find the village an historical sort of place to match?" she said.

They came down into it very shortly after that, and there were certainly cottages that went back two hundred years and more; and an inn that was a perfect picture, with its black oak beams and deep yellow plaster and latticed panes; the whole leaning forward above the narrow village street as though it meant to have a good look at all that went up and down. "Quite a heavenly old place!" Judy thought. " *What* a pity our old lady had

147

to stop at the windmill! This would have been nicer for her to rest in, and then we could all have explored and had tea and no end of a time."

They felt more sorry than ever that their travelling companion had not been able to manage that last mile and a half, when they had found the post office, the walk to which led them past one of the beautiful dignified old churches so usual in Sussex.

It would have been so exciting to wait the answer to the wire at Lulliston and spend the time exploring. But, as it was, duty called them back to the tired old lady, and Maura's wire explained as nearly as possible the spot where the accident had happened, and said that she and Judy were now going back to the train.

They bought three dejected-looking buns and a bag of bull's-eyes at the little general shop which combined itself with the post office, and then prepared to make their best pace back to the windmill, only turning a little aside to let their way back take them through the church-yard, so that they should see just a little of the history of this dear old place.

They were very hasty glances that they gave to right and left, for the old lady lay heavy on their consciences; they got a general notion of a magnificent tower with Norman arches, a heavy weather-beaten lych gate, a tall wooden cross commemorating a whole boat's crew lost at sea—and something else.

It was Judy who caught sight of that something else and made a hasty excursion in its direction, heedless of Maura's call: "Come on; I'm getting hungry, and we can't eat our buns here."

"Half a minute," Judy sent back; "go on, Maura; I'll run after you." And Judy reached the headstone that had caught her attention.

It was an old headstone, slanting heavily like all the others, and with the lettering upon it half obliterated by time, weather, and the spreading lichen. The grave that it commemorated had once been enclosed within a railed square; but the chief part of the railing had fallen away, and only a little remained to show that the grave had been well cared for once upon a time. The grave or graves—for as Judy looked more closely she saw that another mound lay, curiously placed, across the foot of the first, the head of which was marked by that dim tombstone—were in the centre of that square, and the space around them was there still, though overgrown with nettles. With a queer and inexplicable thrill of excitement, Judy knelt down beside the headstone and scraped away a little of the lichen with her Guide knife which she had loose in the pocket of her coat.

She had begun the clearing process at the bottom of the lettering, not at the top; and the first letters readable were, "——bina, his wife."

"Bina—what a queer name," Judy thought, and scraped away a little more of the grey lichen. A name faced her quite distinctly then. " *Jacobina, his wife.*" And then Judy knew that she was on the brink of a discovery.

She scraped recklessly, heedless of Maura's impatient calls from the lych gate, and got the lettering clear at last, or at least as clear as time and weather working their will for over two hundred years allowed.

"Beneath this stone lie, in sure and certain hope
of a Joyful Resurrection, the mortal remains of
CHARLES LUCIAN BETHUNE,
who suffered on Tower Hill 2nd February, 1716.
' My trust is in the tender mercy of
God for ever and ever.'
Also at his feet, according to her desire, Jacobina,
his Wife."

Judy knelt on the grass regardless of the nettles amongst
it and looked and looked. She did not hear Maura; her
mind was back in the past—a past of over two hundred
years ago.

Poor little namesake ancestress who could not, it
seemed, forgive herself; was she still thinking of the lost
treasure that might, perhaps, have saved her husband,
when she asked to lie humbly at his feet? Anyhow,
Judy hoped that the text upon the tombstone had been
her choice and her comfort.

Until Uncle Jimmy had showed her those family
papers yesterday, Judy had known practically nothing
of her family history. She had been little more than a
baby when her father was killed in the war, and she
and her mother went to live with a school friend of her
mother's, who possessed a purse bigger than she needed,
away in the Orkneys, and the old friend went on taking
care of Judy when her mother died of pneumonia after
only three days' illness. It was then that Uncle Jimmy
had come all the long journey north to see his niece,
and had told her that he would take care of her, and have
her to live with him as soon as he could have a house of
his own again. He had taken care very faithfully;
remittances came regularly to cover the expenses of Judy's

keep and clothes, and Uncle Jimmy remembered birthdays as well as Christmas. But the house of his own was yet to find, and Judy had only come to share Mrs. Petticum's lodgings with him because Mrs. M'Kay couldn't keep her any longer.

Now, for the first time, she realised that somewhere near Lulliston must have stood the gracious old manor house of the Bethunes, which had passed from hands too poor to hold it; and that the inn she and Maura had so admired was probably the very inn where that other Jacobina had entered her coach, because even her courage quailed at stepping into it at the manor doors. And, of course, how could she have forgotten? It was Ritchling Common over which that other Jacobina had been joggling and jolting on the way to the Assembly, when Hare Lambert and his confederates stopped her coach and helped themselves to the Bethune emeralds. The block on the line had resulted in a look back into the past for Judy Bethune.

Maura, slightly exasperated, was marching combatively towards her, still nursing the untouched bag of buns.

"Are you *never* coming, Judy? I'm half starved, and so, I'm sure, is our old lady."

Judy gave a great jump; of course, it wasn't fair to explore here any longer because she happened to have found something that was so very interesting to herself. Perhaps, when Uncle Jimmy came down from Scotland, he could be induced to come and fetch her from the Briarlys', and then he and she together could make a pilgrimage to Lulliston, without having to consider anybody else.

But for the present she scrambled off the grass in a

hurry, distinctly apologetic. "I'm ever so sorry, old thing; abominable of me, I know! I'll come at once."

They turned their backs on the quaint old church and churchyard and set off for the windmill at a good round pace, devouring their buns as they went. The bun intended for their travelling companion remained in the bag.

CHAPTER XXIV

RATHER ASTONISHING

THE old lady was no longer standing or sitting in the shadow of the windmill. The girls walked all round it without seeing anything of her. The coat still lay in the shadow of the windmill, just as they had left it.

"She's gone inside, I expect," suggested Judy. "It's uncommonly hot."

Considering the pace that she and Maura had come up the hill from Lulliston, it was not surprising that they found it so; it was one of those windless summer afternoons which often seem at their hottest above five o'clock. The old half ruined windmill, standing tall and gaunt against the deep blue sky, seemed almost to simmer with the heat.

"I oughtn't to have stayed so long in the churchyard," Judy murmured with compunction, mopping her scarlet face with her handkerchief. "Grown-ups get frightfully ill with the heat, I know, especially if they're rather aged."

"She would have been better with me, resting hours at the lych gate, while you mooned over tombstones," grinned Maura. "But don't you worry yourself, Judy, you old mugwump; come along inside. It's gorgeously cool in there, I expect, and if we weren't first-class idiots we should never have expected the poor old thing to stay grilling outside the round-house."

Judy followed her friend into what was left of the

153

round-house, a low one-storeyed building, painted black, that formed as it were an outer belt to the tall windmill; only a belt that surrounded its foot, not its waist.

Inside the round-house it was certainly cool and much more roomy than Judy would have expected. But it was also exceedingly dark, coming from the glare outside, and both girls stood blinking in the darkness and with very little chance, it seemed at first, of seeing if the old lady was there.

"I wish we knew her name," Maura whispered. "Can't think why she didn't tell us; we told ours very early on."

"They don't tell things the same way when they're a good deal grown-up. But I wish we did know, specially as it's so dark. It seems so jolly rude to call, ' Are you there? ' without saying any name, and yet how can we when we don't know any," Judy said.

"Don't do that; yell out, ' We're here—Judy and Maura,'" was Maura's resourceful idea.

Judy having nothing better to suggest, they followed it; and between them they certainly made a considerable noise and the echoes repeated it, but there was no response from their old lady. During their absence in Lulliston, she seemed to have vanished from the face of the earth.

"How queer!" Judy said at last, standing in the centre of the building and looking upwards. "I suppose she must have gone back to the train, for she couldn't have climbed those ladders."

"I doubt if anybody could now," Maura remarked, examining the ladders leading to the first floor of the windmill. "They look ever so ancient and rotten."

"Suppose I just shin up a little way to make sure there's nothing to find out above?" Judy suggested, not sorry to have a reasonable reason for exploring with a slight risk to add zest. "I'm not much weight; the ladders won't be too rotten to bear me."

"Well, don't go farther than the first floor," Maura begged, rather doubtfully, for she was nearly a year Judy's senior, and not at all too sure about the safety of the ladders, even for the undeniably light weight of her friend. Only she knew from experience that Judy was not easy to dissuade when she had made up her mind to anything, and to suggest that it might be dangerous would probably incite her to further explorations.

"Right-o!" Judy agreed cheerfully, and was away up the first ladder like a lamp-lighter, landing quite safely on the first floor, for all that more than one rung of rotting ladder had come away under her feet *en route.*

It was a good deal lighter on the first floor than it had been down below, for all the wide gap where once had been the round-house door. But here above, though the windows were little more than slits, time and weather had made other openings, through which Judy could see the gaunt skeleton of what once had been the great sails of the mill.

"What's it like?" shrieked Maura from below, in tones which must have roused the deafest old lady had she been anywhere in hearing, and Judy shouted back: "Dusty and birds'-nesty and—and awfully nice!"

It certainly was an attractive place partly perhaps because the light came into it in streaks, for that seemed to catch certain objects and make them stand out most mysteriously. Judy would have liked to invite her friend to come up and share the fun, but it was well known at Miss Salway's school that Maura Briarly had no head for heights, though she was always a sport about anything. And the ladders were rotten as well as steep, and Maura was a good deal bigger and nearly a year older than herself. No, the only thing to be done was to do an exploration that was extremely rapid and get down to Maura again.

The long shafts of sunlight showed a great deal of dust and a great deal of emptiness, and a bent and battered corned beef tin and one old boot, with sole and uppers gaping asunder, and nothing else very particular. Certainly no trace of the missing old lady. Ladders that went up higher and appeared to be even more rotten than those she had ascended; a smell of must and dust, and—something else. For, as Judy kicked the empty corned beef tin a little to one side, wishing that there could have been something a little more thrilling to find now she had come up, she saw something scrawled quite plainly on the dirty floor beneath it—the figure "5," and below the figure, an odd mark like this, *X*. Only, the mark was not made with chalk as the figure was, but with tiny twigs broken off. And as she lifted one she saw that the twigs were quite fresh with the sap hardly dried in them.

"I wonder who on earth put those twigs there, and why?" Judy asked herself, staring down at her find. But there was no answer. The curious arrangements of twigs might easily have been child's play; only there seemed to be no cottages near, and Judy did not fancy that children would be encouraged to climb up and down those rotting ladders in any case.

She pushed aside the rest of the rubbish, but without finding anything else of the least interest. Maura's calls from below became very insistent, and with a final look round at the place which held the unfulfilled promise

of mystery she scrambled down the ladders again to find
the long-suffering Maura really rather annoyed.

"I never knew anybody like you for sticking in places,
Judy. Our old lady clearly isn't here, and you'll find
we'll miss the train if you don't hurry a bit more—it's
well after five already.

"After five!" cried Judy. Her watch had stopped—a
not unusual occurrence. Then she began to laugh; then
she stopped herself and told her friend what she had
found upstairs.

"Pure coincidence," she cried; "at least it's sure to be,
but let's have a good look below, train or no train.
Then we shan't go worrying ourselves afterwards and
wondering if there was anything special about ' 5 '."

They had neither matches nor torch and the round-
house was no lighter than it had been. Judy thought
indignantly that in a book the sun's rays should have
slanted in at exactly the convenient angle and showed
them all they wanted at the exact moment they most
wanted it. But after the comparative light of the floor
above, the round-house seemed particularly dim, and
five might have been chalked all over the place without
the two girls being any the wiser.

Judy thought of the convenient openings above and
felt the round-house wall with both hands. "Only wood;
it ought to be giving somewhere?"

"Judy, you ass! Look out, we'll be had up for dam-
aging property," objected Maura.

"Who's going to damage anything? I'm only finding
out if anything is loose."

A bit of rotten wood gave under her hand—a long
shaft of sunset peered through the hole it left. And it
showed the thrilled Judy four little twigs together,

almost under her feet, as she stood there; four little twigs laid together in precisely the same pattern as the others had been, though surrounded and half overlaid by a litter of twigs that might have been thrown down carelessly by some child playing, or might have been put there of intent. "Maura, do come along and look at this; it's so queer!" Judy cried.

Together the two girls looked, on hands and knees on the dusty round-house floor, for in spite of the openings that Judy had made it couldn't be described as light in the round-house. But you certainly see more if your head is close to the floor, and above all, when you are expecting—or at least half expecting—that there will be something to see.

Judy caught the line in the dust before Maura, but Maura it was who suggested that a slab might tip up, if it had no iron ring with which to lift it. The dust had been disturbed, even the dim light made that sure when they came to look, and the floor was paved with stone flags. "A flag ought to lift; it would in a book," Maura said; and they pushed and pulled hopefully, and felt sure that they were on the brink of a discovery.

But the flags all about the area where the twigs were dropped and dust disturbed seemed quite immovable, and even Maura's faith in the adventure gave way at last.

She stood up. "Come on, Judy; I don't believe there's anything in it."

"What about the crossed twigs?" Judy wanted to know, still pounding and tugging.

"Aren't you fed up with this place? I am."

"Oh, wait another sec. or so!"

"Right-o," Maura said resignedly. She was standing before the ladder; she raised her hands above her head and grasped the highest rung that she could reach. "Hurry up, Sherlock Holmes!" she implored, in accents that spelt boredom, and swung sideways, hanging by her hands. "Not such a bad way of doing gym," she said, bending her body to give impetus to another swing.

"Look out—the rungs are rotten," Judy called out.

"Not far to fall if they are," sang Maura, keeping time to her words with her swinging. "I've got to do something, haven't I, while you grub about on the floor!"

There was a sudden, terrific crash, as Maura and the ladder came down together, falling sideways, and missing the crouching Judy by about the third of an inch. The ladder buckled against the wall and drove a hole right through it, the other end, forced hard against the floor by the momentary resistence of the stout tarred wall, tilted the stone flag at which the two girls had worked in vain. It opened almost under Judy's knees, and she all but went into the square hole which had been brought to view with such dramatic suddenness.

Maura, crawling from underneath the buckled ladder, shaken but only slightly bruised, gave a wild whoop of joy when she saw what her gymnastics had achieved.

"Cheerio, Judy; we've got our secret passage after all."

CHAPTER XXVII

A SMUGGLERS' BURROW

THE two girls peered over into the dark hole with much excitement. They ought probably to have thought very penitently about the mischief they had done in tearing a ladder from its moorings and sending it crashing through a wall, but they didn't. It must be owned that they thought of nothing but the opening in the floor.

"It must be one end of a secret passage, of course," Maura screamed, forgetting all about her fright and bruises.

"We must go down it—a little way anyhow," Judy urged, in an equal state of excitement. "Fancy finding a real thrilling secret passage of our own; what does it matter if the train does go on without us after that? Do you think Christopher Columbus would have worried about trifles when he was discovering America?"

"There weren't any trains to worry about," Maura mentioned practically, "but I quite agree, Judy, what does anything matter? Besides, I expect Daddy will send for us; and if he doesn't find us by the train he'll drive round, making weird noises on the horn until I yell an answer."

And having disposed of all objections very comfortably, the two proceeded to climb down into the dark opening.

It was very thrilling; it was also rather difficult and a little dangerous. There were steps of a kind, or rather, uneven holes in the side of a wall, but these were rather broken away, and there seemed little to which to hold. Still, slipping, scrambling, laughing—the two girls got down somehow, and arrived on firm ground in a place that was dark and low and rather fusty.

"Oh, I think it's lovely," Judy cried enthusiastically. "Just the kind of smell that goes with smugglers' passages and mysterious sounds and hollow caves and . . ."

"Will you shut up! You're trying to frighten me," Maura said firmly. "I wish your blessed smugglers had left us a light as well as a mouldy smell."

"It would have been handy," agreed Judy. "Still, never mind—we can fumble along. I'm touching a wall now—let's keep by that and then we know we can always get back if we want."

Maura was in reality no less keen than her friend was, though she thought it the due of her eleven months' seniority to laugh a little at Judy's enthusiasms.

"All right," she agreed, "but if you announce the discovery of any mouldering bones or cheerful little finds of that sort, don't expect me to be pleased, that's all."

Judy in front and Maura following close, they made their way some dozen yards down the low, dark passage, feeling by the wall. And then Judy suddenly stopped short with a start that had dismay in it, communicating itself to her friend at once.

"What—what is it?" Maura demanded.

"I walked against something."

"Something what?"

"It was soft like clothes," Judy whispered, wishing that she could keep her teeth from chattering. It was all very well to talk lightly about mouldering bones as part of the ordinary furniture of a smugglers' passage when you never expected for one instant to see any; it was quite another thing to stumble into what felt like a bundle of clothes in the stuffy, frightening dark, with sunshine and the outdoor world ever so far away, and to know, if you were not going to write yourself down the coward a Guide must not be, you must nerve yourself to find out what the thing was.

Together the two girls felt over the bundle. Clothes certainly—something beaded about them by the feel; then something hard and cold. Judy, who had come up against it, recoiled instinctively; could it be a human bone? One of those of which she and Maura had thought and spoken so cheerfully.

Then she put out her hand resolutely and took it up; one must have the pluck to find out.

She turned it about in her hand; it was heavy, but Judy supposed bones were that. Something stuck out towards one end of it; she pushed at it with her thumb, wondering whether it belonged or was something clinging to the bone; and—a welcome but very startling blaze of light shone out dazzlingly, making the two girls gasp and blink. And it was no bone that they held, but a small and narrow electric torch, which would seem to have been left in the pocket, now pulled inside out, of a long black skirt which had, somehow, a familiar look to both girls.

They stared at it, then at the other clothes, in horrified amazement. There could be no sort of doubt about it, these were the clothes at which they had looked in the train during that journey which had ended so unexpectedly; this was the skirt they had seen held up above elastic-sided boots as the three marched over Ritchling Common in search of a post office. They had stumbled on a bundle of their old lady's garments down there in the darkness of the secret passage.

For a whole minute neither spoke. Then Judy, in an awestruck whisper, and glancing over her shoulder, said: "Maura, do you think she has been murdered?"

"She doesn't look the sort of old lady any one would murder," Maura contributed, holding on desperately to common sense. "Judy, why should they?"

"I don't know." Judy was a little cheered by Maura's point of view. "And anyhow, it would be frightfully odd to take off her dress and cloak before they did it. Murderers are always supposed to be in a hurry."

"But where can she be?" Maura stood up, and, taking the torch from Judy, held it now high, now low, trying to get an idea of this underground place. The girls now saw it to be low, not very wide, and tunnelling away to the far end, opposite to that by which they had come in.

"It's a passage right enough," Maura said; "and it's too narrow for any one to be hidden here, where we are, without our seeing them."

"Then she must be farther along," Judy said, getting to her feet and giving herself a little shake. "We had better get along at once and look for her."

"Yes," Maura agreed, almost valiantly.

"We can't let anything have happened to her and not go along to see about it," Judy remarked by way of a further stiffener to courage. "After all, as you say, there would be no reason to murder her. She's probably shut up, a prisoner somewhere, because she stumbled on some thrilling smuggler mystery."

"But why did they make her take her dress off?" Maura wanted to know.

"Oh, perhaps they decided to disguise her, for some

reason," Judy suggested. "That's it, Maura, you bet; and we shall find her a prisoner, gagged and bound and dressed quite differently, in some secret place. . . ."

"They couldn't disguise her much," Maura said, with half a chuckle. "'Member her curls? They're a bit unique."

"Unless they cut them off," said Judy, warming to her theory.

"Then they'll be with the clothes; we'd better look." Judy flung herself upon her knees by the black bundle —rummaging, shaking—while Maura held the torch down to throw light upon the scene. They had nearly given it up, for the pocket was empty, when something shook out of one of the sleeves of the old-fashioned bodice —some little fleecy white curls, with a neat invisible hairpin sticking in each.

The girls examined them carefully by the light of the torch, then laughed outright.

"My word, so they weren't her own? Shouldn't have said she would go in for such pomps and vanities," Judy said. "We mustn't let out that we found them when we find her."

"No-o," Maura agreed; "but it does strike me, Judy, there is a bit of a mystery about this."

"Well, let's get on and solve it," Judy cried impatiently. "It's no use sitting here and saying how odd it all is. We've got to look after the poor old soul if she does wear false hair—I suppose?"

"Yes," agreed Maura slowly. She was thinking, and she followed Judy in silence, as her junior marched determinedly on ahead into the passage, carrying the torch. Maura was fifteen and had had more experience in many way than Judy: she was not quite happy about the situation, even though she believed that no murder had been done. She knew afterwards that it was then she began to feel a little doubtful about the old lady, though her suspicions were too vague and nebulous for putting into words.

They went along the passage, Judy marching in front with the torch, burning to find and release a forcibly disguised and captive old lady; and Maura following, rather unhappy, because she was wondering all the time if they ought to be doing any such thing.

But Judy, troubled with no doubts, went gaily on at a pace which nearly landed her upon her nose more than once, for after the beginning, which had been fairly level, the passage was on a considerable slope.

It was less stuffy than might have been expected, for though in general the roof was low, there were places where it seemed to arch upward to a considerable height, and in these the girls noticed there always seemed to be a whistle of fresh air; still, it was not a particularly pleasant place to walk in.

Stumbling and slipping, the two girls had struggled on for a considerable distance without seeing any sign of their old lady, when there was rather a startling sound to hear just then—a sound of footsteps coming heavily towards them. Men's footsteps, certainly, and more than one man, by the sound.

Judy backed on Maura, treading rather hard upon her foot. Then both girls stood quite still, listening breathlessly. It had occurred to Judy as well as to Maura that their presence in the passage might need a little explaining, especially if their fellow-occupants of the passage were the kind of people who indulge in such pastimes as kidnapping old ladies.

CHAPTER XXXI

ONE MYSTERY SOLVED

THEY had a choice of three things—to face it out—to bolt back to the upper air—to find a hiding place.

Neither was really particularly keen to face it out until they had a little idea as to the sort of people who were coming stealthily up the smugglers' passage towards them, and it was a long way back to the flagstone in the round-house, and if they ran for it, it was more than possible that the men would do the same, and very possibly catch them.

The third alternative naturally involved a question —was there any sort of hiding place to be found? The men presumably would have a torch. It wouldn't do just to flatten against the wall and trust to luck.

And everything had to be decided so quickly. By the sound the men could not be far away.

Maura confessed afterwards to a wild idea of trying to cover the two of them with the old lady's voluminous skirt, as it lay huddled on the path, but that meant going a good way back, even if the clothes could be expected to cover girls of fourteen and fifteen, and still look in the least bit like a harmless bundle lying on the ground.

It was Judy who realised that they were in one of those sections of the passage where the roof rose higher. She swept her torch above her head to see if there were any hiding places, and saw that to the right the path widened, and where the widening came was a dark hole half-way up the wall.

She darted across. It was about six feet up, not very large about the mouth, but large enough, she thought, for Maura and herself, with a squeeze.

There was not a second to be lost. "Get up on my shoulder—quick!" she whispered to Maura, bracing herself against the wall, and Maura obeyed, clutching at the opening of the hole, and sending down on her friend's head a shower of earth and small stones. She was big enough and strong enough to pull up the lighter and more active Judy by the hands, and they crouched most uncomfortably in the hole, which seemed to slope down to a depth they did not dare explore just then.

Judy extinguished the torch, and they listened breathlessly to steps that were now so near that they had horrid doubts lest their hasty movements should have been heard.

The slow, cautious scrunching grew near and louder. They could distinguish subdued voices; a faint light, growing stronger, began to illumine the path, and then three men came into sight.

The torch carried by the middle one was a good deal larger and stronger than the pocket one that Judy and Maura had been using; in fact, it was stronger than the two girls quite appreciated, considering how easy it would be, if it were switched a little farther round, to light up their hiding place.

But at present it was held low to light the path. That was a comfort, though it would have been interesting if they could have seen a little more of the three men who shared their smugglers' passage with them. But at least they could hear them, and what they heard was really quite as interesting as anything they could have seen.

The man in the centre, who held the torch, did not speak at first. He appeared to be listening to the other two, and they were very busy impressing something upon him, it seemed to the two eavesdroppers in the hiding-hole. But since it is always difficult to pick up conversation in the middle of it, when you have not the least notion what has gone before, they didn't catch the drift of it at first.

"Dead high at 9—then we can float the boat out from the cave."

"There'll be none too much time though."

"Lucky the old lady got the chance of her gentle little stroll to give us the news when she did."

Judy just suppressed a gasp of excitement. News was coming of their friendly old lady at last. So it was, though not quite in the way she expected.

For the man in the centre answered that remark, which was made with a kind of grim chuckle, and he answered it in a voice that was strangely familiar.

"Yes, but the meeting with the innocent pair of kids in search of a travelling companion was our biggest stroke of luck. Craddock of the Yard, nosing round at Victoria, would have had me when he came past the window, I believe, if he had ever dreamt he would see me in charge of little schoolgirls. And, of course, the block on the line was most uncommonly handy too. I had the jimjams about getting out at Ritchling, when my two defenders were going on to Dunsterby. As it was, their desire to look for post offices just suited me, and long may they look! ... By the way, I hope you didn't leave anything about for them to spot when they come back to see if I'm still here—they wear the Girl Guide badge, I see, and that seems to mean such terribly observant youngsters. . . ."

The three men passed on, still talking, but with their voices dying away into distance. The listeners had certainly managed to hear a good deal of themselves this time, but it might have been good, bad, or indifferent for all they thought about it just then. For the voice which had come from the middle man was without any doubt the voice of the old lady about whose fate they had suffered such anxiety!

The audience of two had the sense to keep absolute silence until by the sounds they were certain that the men were out of earshot, though it was distinctly severe exercise in self-control, considering that the men appeared to be heading at a good pace for the opening, and when they found it open, would know at once that some one had come down into the passage, and guess it to be the "observant youngsters."

Judy spoke first. "My word! We've gone and done it!"

She giggled. "That old lady did spoof us jolly well, didn't she?"

Maura gave her an indignant poke.

"Judy, don't be an ass! It's really rather serious. It's no good chortling like that as though it were a joke. We've got to think what's to be done!"

Judy straightened her face with difficulty. "What do you think they're doing? They can't be burgling down here—there's nothing to burgle."

"I don't know, but they're doing something criminal, I believe," Maura said. "Did you hear our old lady—

man, I mean, say about Craddock of the Yard? The Yard means Scotland Yard, you know."

"O-oh! Think they're gun-running?" suggested Judy.

"They're going to float something out of a cave at 9—that is the time when the tide is right, I suppose," said Maura thoughtfully. "I wonder what we ought to do?"

Judy grinned. "There isn't much choice, is there, seeing they're between us and the opening. I don't take it they would be so wildly delighted to meet us, you know. We shall just have to go on, and in the course of going, with any luck, we ought to land on the solution of mystery number two—what they're doing in the burrow. I must say I should like to know that."

"All right," Maura agreed. "I suppose it is safe now, and I shan't be sorry to get out of this hole, for one. It's so slopy and slippy, and the sides keep crumbling under my feet."

"Well, here goes! Let us get out," Judy said.

She got as firm a grip as possible and dug in her toes. "Here! Mind! You're sending down piles of earth on me," objected Maura.

"Sorry—oh, here's a big stone wedged—I'll grip on to that," Judy declared, handing down the torch to Maura, just behind her.

The big stone was to the right of the opening. It was certainly a very big stone, and should afford the firm hold which Judy was finding it rather difficult to get elsewhere. In all the excitement of discussing the situation, she had let herself slip rather far down into the hole, and, as Maura said, the soil was crumbling, and she could not help showering a good deal down upon her friend. But she could pull herself up by the hands quite easily if there were only something on which to pull. The stone seemed beautifully firm. Judy grabbed at the bit which stuck out. At the same moment, Maura hung on to her suddenly. "Wait! They're coming back!"

The stone was by no means so firmly wedged as it appeared to be. Judy was pulling on it hard, to get the necessary impetus to bring her knees up to the opening, without driving her toes into the crumbling side of the hole. Maura's weight coming upon her unexpectedly —and it was her full weight, for the dash to stop Judy from jumping out into the passage had destroyed her rather precarious balance—did not make her lose her hold of the stone, but it did something else, and worse— it loosened the stone from its foundation.

An avalanche of earth seemed to rush upon Judy, bearing her down with it—her eyes, mouth and nose seemed full of earth—something crashed past her, without touching her, and both the girls were lying, Maura undermost, down at the bottom of a pitch dark pit!

CHAPTER XXIX

THE AMAZING DISCOVERY

Judy was the first to recover. Choking and coughing, she managed to wriggle herself a little clear of poor Maura and to realise that she herself seemed to have escaped undamaged, except for a grazed knee and elbow.

What about Maura though? Judy was beginning to guess what had happened. The huge stone must have come out with their united tug and have caused something of an earthslide. Lucky indeed for the pair of them that it had been wedged so much to the side of the opening, Judy reflected. It must have just missed them in its downward slide, and what had borne them down was the weight of loosened earth that had followed its removal.

But for all she realised that the stone had missed them, Judy was horribly afraid for Maura, and it made everything so much worse that it was all in pitchy darkness. Maura had been holding the torch, but where it might have fallen nobody could guess.

"Maura!" Judy got out, after a little more choking and coughing. "Maura! You're not hurt! Do try just to say something! *Maura!*"

She knelt down by her friend on the yielding, fallen earth, and felt her over cautiously, with a thudding heart.

Maura was lying in a sort of crumpled heap. Judy straightened her out with difficulty, for Maura was a good deal bigger than she was and seemed extraordinarily heavy.

It was horrid to have her lying there like that without making a sound. Poor Judy groped round desperately in the thick, black, frightening darkness for the torch. Not in either of Maura's clutched hands—they were full of earth, but no torch was in either. Of course, it wasn't likely that she would be holding it still. It was probably somewhere underneath the fall of earth, and that, luckily, was not thick.

Judy started to dig as best she could, scraping up earth with her hands to the great detriment of her nails. Somehow or another she must find that torch, or how could she see what was wrong with Maura, or find a way out of this pit for them both.

Judy dug for that torch under difficulties. She had no idea before how difficult it would be to judge depth or anything in the dark. She scraped out a hole, and thought she had reached hard earth into which the torch would scarcely have gone, and started again in another place and got to a hard strata much sooner this time, and wondered if she had really got to it before, or only fancied she had, and felt for the old hole to make sure, and found it and then lost the other, and had to start again somewhere else. It looked as though it might take days to find that torch. Judy supposed she ought to try and map out the area so as to be sure she went all over it, only it was such a difficult thing to do in the thick dark, and when you were terribly frightened about your friend.

When she had dug without result till her hands were sore, for what seemed hours but probably was about twenty minutes, she decided that she must raise a shout and bring even mysterious and possibly furious criminals to her help. Judy was not really much afraid of anybody, but she was very much afraid of what might happen to her friend if nothing was done for her.

If it had occurred to her to shout at once, instead of waiting to hunt for the torch, she might possibly have been heard; and the ending of this story would have been a very different one. For, as it happened, about twenty minutes before, three men *were* standing in the passage, quite near the spot where the girls had taken cover, holding a somewhat agitated council. But they were well out of hearing of the weak little voice, which, to her disgust, was all that Judy found she could produce by the time she started to call; and her shouts died away into a faint, exhausted squeak, unanswered.

Poor Judy waited for a minute or two to pull herself together, and then made another feverish search for the torch. Failing to find it, she made two attempts to climb the side of the pit in search of the help which she must manage to get for Maura.

She gave that up after the second attempt, however, because the earth would crumble and slip away under her feet, and she was desperately afraid of bringing another slide down on poor Maura. So she slithered to the bottom of the pit again, and groped her way to her friend and crouched down by her, feeling miserable. But feeling miserable was not a bit of help; she knew that she must get on to it and do something. So she rolled over on her face and began that dreary task of digging and scooping with sore smarting fingers all over again. If she went on scratching up the fallen soil long enough she must come upon the torch in time.

She worked on, stiffening her courage; she must find that torch if she scraped away the earth for hours and hours, and absolutely skinned her fingers in the process!

Here at last was what felt like something hard; of course it might only be the cover of a stone, but then again it might not. She scraped on more hopefully; by the feel of the spot she almost thought that the big stone, which was very near, must have pushed a sort of furrow in the earth, before settling itself. The torch might easily have rolled into this furrow, Judy thought. Lucky that the ground was so soft and churned up, there would be quite a good chance that it wasn't smashed!

It was certainly odd and tiresome of it to have gone in so far, but Judy worked now with hope in her heart, and felt as though at least half her troubles would have rolled away if she could only see light, blessed light again!

Something hard under her burrowing fingers certainly, and not a stone: it didn't feel the least bit like a stone, as she got farther down to it. There seemed to be something soft and puzzling with it, too—something that seemed rotten and gave way as she tried to pull the hard thing up by it. She had to go back patiently to her laborious scraping: she didn't want to stop, even though the mysterious something felt less and less like the torch she so wanted.

She got it clear at last; it was something long and cold and supple. She sat back on her heels, feeling it over, and her foot clinked on something metal.

Dropping the queer find in her excitement, she swung round, without moving her foot, and grasped—the torch; the torch that she had been hunting for so long. *Was* it damaged?

A touch on the switch with an earthy finger that trembled with eagerness, and a circle of glorious light shone around her, showing a pit with sloping sides and various holes grubbed untidily in the loose earth; a big stone which had ploughed a deep scoop in its path, and —flung carelessly down beside it, amid remnants of some rotten red material, a great necklace of magnificent emeralds, set in tarnished gold!

Judy sat staring down at that strange find of hers, wondering whether she was really asleep and dreaming, when—behind her—Maura's voice spoke rather dazedly: "Judy, what's up?"

Judy forgot even her amazing discovery for the moment. "*Maura!* Oh, I *am* glad! Are you all right?"

Her voice broke a little; it was such a wonderful relief to hear Maura speaking, after the long deadly silence.

"Don't be a silly ass; of course I'm all right," Maura assured her bracingly. "My head feels a bit swimming, that's all."

"I'm so frightfully glad you're all right, old thing." Judy told her, a shade huskily. "I thought you mightn't be, you know."

"Ass!" exclaimed Maura witheringly. She looked round with awakening interest.

"What a weird spot! Did we fall down? Yes, I remember now; the stone gave way. Luckily it didn't land on top of us; you would have had some reason for thinking I was done for then. But, you poor kid, it must have been rather beastly for you before I started jawing; was it long? And, I say, were you amusing yourself playing at being a puppy digging up bones?"

Maura had seen the holes.

Judy recovered herself; there certainly wasn't very much the matter with Maura. She plunged across to the big stone on hands and knees.

"Stop ragging, and just have a squint at what I *did* dig up," she announced, with a touch of boastfulness that was perhaps excusable under the circumstances. "I was hunting for that old torch—and got this!"

She held the necklace up: through the soil clinging to them the wonderful gems caught the torch's rays and sparkled gloriously.

"My word!" was all the breathless Maura could say.

"Yes, some find, isn't it?" Judy exulted; "and, do you know, Maura, I can't help thinking that the necklace is the very one my ancestress, the other Jacobina, lost, more than two hundred years ago."

"*What?*" Maura shrieked; and Judy very briefly gave the outline of the story told her by Uncle Jimmy only yesterday morning in Mrs. Petticum's lodgings, and of the grave in the churchyard near by, the grave with the strange inscription.

"That other Jacobina lived close here, and it was over her Ritchling Common that we came," she concluded. "I believe this place we're in was a smugglers' burrow thenadays, and that we're on the track of all the Bethune emeralds at last."

Maura promptly forgot her aching head, and both were equally forgetful of the advisibility of escaping from their rather stuffy prison as fast as possible.

"Come on! Let's dig some more," Maura urged, and they dug. It was, of course, ever so much easier now that they had light to guide them and the knowledge within a quite small area of where to work.

They took turns to scrape up earth and to hold the light, and the hunt was so exciting that no one minded her digging turn.

Scraps of worm-eaten, rotting, red stuff kept appearing: the jewels had once been carefully wrapped up, no doubt, probably in a voluminous red handkerchief. Then Judy pricked herself severely with the sharp point of a brooch, shaped like a star, with emerald points and a great diamond blazing in the centre. Soon after Maura found two emerald-set bracelets, made for a very slender wrist. But it was Judy who made the discovery which was, in some ways, the most exciting of all.

It was a dirty square of very thick coarse paper which may once have been white. Now it was stained a dirty yellow and felt rotten to their touch. But the quaint cramped characters upon it, though blurred, were still readable, and the girls deciphered them together by the light of the torch.

" *The curse of the witch of Marsdyke is hereby bought by Hare Lambert, and paid fair and honest, that the emeralds be hid safe till pursuit be turned away and he can fetch them again. The black pox is laid upon any meddling wi' 'em, the creeping sickness, and the grey crone's ill luck on aught and any that be his'n.*

" *This curse I, the witch of Marsdyke, lay on any touching what Hare Lambert took and hid; saving only the rightful owner of the jewels, where my curse can't lie.*"

Maura looked round a little nervously, as though she half expected to see the awful curse for which Hare Lambert had paid long ago take some horrible bodily shape beyond the cheering circle of the torch-light.

But Judy laughed triumphantly. "Don't you see Maura, we're the right ones to find them? I'm a Bethune, and these *are* the lost Bethune emeralds, and my Uncle Jimmy's own."

CHAPTER XXX

NOT QUITE SO SIMPLE

THE mysterious men and their problematical proceedings had receded into the far distance for the time being; you can't think about everything at once, and the discovery of the lost Bethune emeralds was rather a large-sized thing to think about. Indeed, Judy had started quite calmly to clean the necklace with her sleeve, which wasn't improved by the process. It was Maura who noticed that the light of the electric torch was growing perceptibly dimmer.

"I say, we had better be thinking of getting out of this," she suggested. "There's a limit to the time these blessed things burn, isn't there?"

Judy started. To tell truth she had had quite enough of that pit in the dark: though, of course, it wouldn't be so bad now she had companionship.

"Sorry, Maura, I *am* a fool! I suppose we may take it that old train has gone on, but that doesn't matter.

" Once we get out of this airless place we can think what to do."

"On the strength of the family fortune I think you might pay a taxi home, if Daddy doesn't roll up," Maura suggested.

"On the strength of the family fortune I shouldn't think Uncle Jimmy would care what I did," Judy pronounced magnificently. She began to wrap the necklace in her own handkerchief, which had, as was not uncom-

179

mon with Judy's handkerchiefs, seen cleaner days. She
stuffed the handkerchief with its precious and princely
contents into the front of her frock, to leave her hands
free for the climb. Then she pushed in the witch's curse.

"I wonder how you can; I'd leave that," Maura said
disgustedly. "She probably wrote it in her blood, or
something beastly, you know."

"I don't care," Judy informed her callously. "It's a—
historic relic and would thrill the British Museum to its
marrow, and what do her curses matter. *We're* not
thieves!"

"Not thieves perhaps, but *spies*, I think," said a too
familiar voice above their heads. Judy had spoken
loudly in her desire to convince Maura there was nothing
to fear in the witch's curse, and the pit was barely seven
feet in depth. The light of a far stronger torch than
theirs was illuminating their prison, and from the top of
the pit a face was looking down, a face last seen surrounded by bobbing white curls.

Judy was suddenly and uncomfortably conscious of
the bulge in the front of her frock; a minute ago escape
had seemed comparatively simple, for it wouldn't matter
now how much earth she and Maura kicked down, and
now they were caught, by men who were probably
criminals, and she, like that other Jacobina, had all the
Bethune emeralds in her keeping. Only a minute before
Judy had been joyfully picturing Uncle Jimmy away at
Cragailoch, receiving a thrilling telegram that would
mean no more slaving over Latin exercises or the forcing
of unwilling ends to the meeting point as long as ever
he lived. And now—was history going to repeat itself
and another Jacobina to lose the family jewels because
she had spoken incautiously loud?

But Judy had never shown the white feather in all her life, and she wasn't going to begin.

"It's you! Hallo!" she called back. "We found your clothes and curls and were ever so puzzled. Do help us out of this hole like a brick; we're fed up with it."

The keen, dark eyes looked hard at her. "It all sounds very natural and innocent, and I've no personal grudge against you two kids—in fact, you have been quite a convenience to me," their travelling companion informed her. "But, unfortunately, you have managed to see too much."

Maura caught her breath, for all her courage; probably Judy's horrible suggestions of earlier in that eventful evening were in her mind. Judy heard the faint sound, and it stiffened her fighting powers. She had landed Maura in this trouble by waiting to polish up the necklace and then talking loudly; she must get her out of it.

"We haven't seen much of the passage, if that's what you mean," she said, "and, of course, we're dying to see more. But we fell down here."

The man lowered his torch so that its light fell full on Judy's upturned face, scratched and decidedly dirty and a little appealing, despite her valiant efforts to look as though she were only longing to see the other end of the passage. Judy had a dreadful sense that he was seeing right through her frock and the handkerchief of dubious cleanliness that held the jewels, to the wonderful Bethune emeralds themselves.

"You think you can get out of this?" he asked.

"Oh, yes, with a torch," Judy said confidently. "It was the darkness made it so hard before, and then I was afraid of pushing earth down on Maura. She was stunned or something."

The man gave a short laugh. "My mates would say I was a fool to trust you kids, but I will," he said. "You did me a better turn than you'll ever know. I'm busy on a stunt that mustn't be disturbed; you give me your solemn promise, both of you, that you won't say a word to any one about this place, nor travelling down with me, nor anything, till this time to-morrow—that will be seven to-morrow evening—it's just five to seven now. You promise, and I'll put you out of the passage, double-quick, before my mates come back and find you, which won't be healthy for you, I can say."

Judy looked at Maura and Maura looked back at Judy. Judy thought of the emeralds: if three angry men were to set upon Maura and herself, the jewels were nearly certain to be discovered; and probably it would be made impossible in some way for them to give away information.

But, on the other hand, both were quite quick enough to know that what their travelling companion alluded to so airily as "a stunt that mustn't be disturbed," meant some illegal and probably criminal proceeding, and had Guides any right to give their help to it, even by their silence?

"We can't," Judy whispered, and Maura nodded.

Judy spoke up. "Sorry, we can't promise that."

"Then you're a pair of little fools," the man said roughly, "and you can blame yourselves, not me, for what you get."

He turned his head over his shoulder and called "Jack!" impatiently, then waited for a second and fumbled in his pockets.

"On second thought, I'll leave you here while I'm busy," he said, "but I'll take precautions to see you don't

get out, for you may be right in thinking you can,
though I bet you haven't had my training as a sailor."

He came neatly down into the pit, with a swing and
a jump, so as to loosen very little earth in his descent.

He took a bit of cord out of his pocket and set down
his torch. "Hands behind you, young lady, and sharp's
the word," he said to Judy; "and think yourself lucky
I have a kind of liking for you two and don't call in my
mates."

He secured Judy's wrists behind her with naval thor-
oughness; resistance would have been useless in any case,
and Judy was far too sensible to try it now when it
would almost certainly lead to the discovery of the
emeralds. Another minute, and Maura was as much
a prisoner as Judy.

"Now, your handkerchiefs over your eyes, and I don't
think you'll get out to blab," he told them.

Maura's handkerchief was sticking out from her coat
pocket, as it happened; the man snatched at it. She
submitted to be blindfolded without protest, because
she was wondering, as Judy was, what in the world would
happen when he demanded hers?

Both knew in a moment. "Where do you keep yours?"
he asked sharply of Judy.

She kept her head. "I lent you my coat when you
were an old lady," she reminded him, with a rather a
thudding heart.

The man hesitated. Into that moment's hesitation
there came a voice calling something that seemed to end
in "Bert!"

"I shall have to use mine, I suppose," the man said
quickly. Judy had a fancy that he was not very anxious
that his mates should find them in the passage.

He whipped a handkerchief from his pocket and knotted it securely behind Judy's head.

"Lot of fancy digging you've been doing," he remarked, stooping to pick up his torch, as Judy guessed, though she could not see.

"I was hunting for our torch," Judy explained calmly.

"You won't need to do that any more," he explained sardonically, "because I'm taking it off with me."

"You're *not*!" Maura's stoicism almost broke down at that.

The man sounded as though he were a little sorry for her. "It won't make much difference to you; you're in the dark anyway. And I shan't be two hours before I come back and let you both loose and out of the passage; if you'll have the sense, as you will by then, to give your promise for silence."

He was gone; they heard him scrambling up the slopes; they heard earth falling under his footsteps; and then the footsteps grew fainter and died away.

They were left helpless, fast prisoners in the dark, within two hours of the time mentioned, when *something* mysterious was going to happen.

CHAPTER XXXI

THE GLORIOUS END

"THERE's one thing," Maura remarked, in a muffled voice, when the footsteps had died into silence; "if we wanted to make asses of ourselves by crying, we couldn't, because we've no hankies."

Judy woke up. She had been thinking with as much vigour as she put into most of her occupations. "Course not!" she said briskly; "but we're not done in, if it comes to that. We can't untie these old cords—sailors' knots always hold—but we might rub them through on the stone."

"Judy! You've got a brain," Maura exclaimed, with admiration.

They got to work. It wasn't easy, first to find the stone, which seemed to elude them in the thick absolute darkness, until Judy fell right over it and grazed her shins; and then to rub the cords without rubbing off skin. But the stone had some convenient sharp edges and both were determined and plucky; they worked through to the last strand that was breakable.

They stretched cramped arms and undid the tight uncomfortable handkerchiefs. The relief was so wonderful that they almost forgot that they were still quite in the dark.

"Well, he climbed out, so can we," Judy said cheerfully. "If he's a sailor, we're Guides. Come on!"

"Which side?" Maura asked.

That was a poser. "Blest if I know," Judy jerked out. "Oh, of course, I *am* a mugwump; we can tell by the footholes; our man stuck his feet a bit in, you may be sure. Let's feel, and we shall know we're in line with the opening."

They felt. It took some time, of course, but Judy wasn't really worrying about the dark now. And sure enough their man had left distinct traces of his ascent; the pair found them most useful. "And we know it's ' left turn ' when we get out," Judy cheerfully remarked, "so we really don't want his old torch: after all, we did pinch it from him."

After some little difficulty in locating it, they crawled through a hole which seemed to have subsided a good deal on one side since the pulling out of the great stone, and dropped into the passage, and then left-turned and groped their way along.

This last bit of their escape seemed longer and more tedious than all the rest put together; perhaps because the end was in sight; perhaps because it was a long time since they had eaten that bun on the way out of Lulliston and they were beginning to suffer from the effects of the inferior supply of good air in the smugglers' passage. More dead than alive, they staggered up the rough steps, and so into the round-house and free air, that smelt delicious, and the long summer twilight.

They sat down weakly for a minute on the floor, and then broke into a hysterical giggle as each saw in the other the dirtiest and most dilapidated girl that she had ever met. They giggled helplessly for a minute; then Judy pulled herself up.

"Come on! Lulliston Police Station ought to be the next move, I expect."

"Oh, lor'! that awful hill!" murmured poor Maura, but she came.

They hadn't gone ten yards on the road to Lulliston, however, when there was a sound that made Maura stop and clutch Judy's arm dramatically. "*Listen!*"

Clear on the soft evening air it came, the hooting of a motor horn, giving some sort of morse call, "—! —! —!"

"M. M. M.! that's me, *good* old Daddy, he's come for us!" Maura said thankfully. "Judy, I really don't think we *could* have walked much farther."

She shouted and waved an arm above her head. A car with several men in it came into sight and slowed down. One jumped out and hugged Maura.

"My dear child, where *have* you been?"

"We left the train, Daddy," Maura began weakly.

"With an old lady, didn't you?" asked another man, who had followed Mr. Briarly from the car. "Tell me everything, please, young ladies. I'm Craddock of the Yard!"

.   .   .   .

Judy and Maura reached the ending of that most eventful journey at something after ten o'clock, and had to be waked up. But they woke next morning as bright as buttons, and none the worse for their adventure, except for their sore wrists, and nails that looked as though they would never be clean. And, first of all, Judy had the happiness of sending a wire of positively reckless length to Uncle Jimmy at Cragailoch telling him of the finding of the lost jewels; and next they both received the thanks and congratulations of Mr. Craddock, the Scotland Yard detective, for the information which had enabled him and his men to effect the arrest of the little gang of clever criminals who had been using the old smugglers' burrow as a headquarters, most unlikely to be raided, for the manufacture of imitation Treasury notes!

"I was on their track, but they would have got the consignment and plant off with the tide, floated out from Crigg's Hole, if it hadn't been for the pair of you," he said warmly.

Uncle Jimmy sold necklace and bracelets, keeping only the brooch, to make into a pendant for Judy by and by, that the family emeralds should not be quite lost to the House of Bethune. They realised ninety thousand pounds, and Uncle Jimmy thankfully resigned the post of Latin master at Miss Salway's school and his dingy rooms in Mrs. Petticum's lodgings, and came to live with Judy at old Lulliston Manor House before those wonderful summer holidays were ended.

Judy was to go as a boarder to St. Oswyth's, and a two-bed room had been promised her, with Maura.

On the first day at Lulliston, Judy was reprehensibly late for dinner, though Uncle Jimmy, always an understanding person, forbore to scold when he learnt the reason.

Judy had been busy in the churchyard that evening, scraping lichen off an old tombstone and cutting grass that had grown long and rank.

When she had made everything quite tidy she stood looking down at that old tombstone, and the two graves there, with thoughtful eyes.

"Anyhow, it's all right now!" she said.

THE END